the eli

M000032137

ENVY

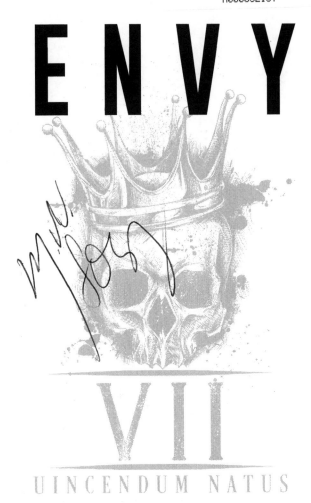

VII

UINCENDUM NATUS

M.N. FORGY

~~lust~~

~~pride~~

~~wrath~~

~~envy~~

greed

gluttony

sloth

ENVY
Copyright © 2019 M.N.FORGY

Cover Design: All By Design
Photo: Adobe Stock
Editor: Word Nerd Editing
Formatting: Champagne Book Design

ALL RIGHTS RESERVED. This book contains material protected under International and Federal Copyright Laws and Treaties. Any unauthorized reprint or use of this material is prohibited. No part of this book may be reproduced or transmitted in any form or by any means, electronic or mechanical, including photocopying, recording, or by an information and retrieval system without express written permission from the Author/Publisher.

This is a work of fiction. Names, characters, places, and incidents either are the product of the author's imagination or are used fictitiously, and any resemblance to actual persons, living or dead, business establishments, events, or locales is entirely coincidental.

Will you love me through thy darkest tales?
It's time to feed my beasts who like their things a little
twisted!

UINCENDUM NATUS

PREFACE

the elite seven

Since 1942, The Elite Seven Society have created and guided influential leaders, molding the country into something better. This society was birthed by Malcom Benedict, II who wanted more for Americans. More wealth. More influence. More power. Some leaders have the skills, but not the influence, and that simply wasn't fair according to Mr. Benedict. He invested his own money and time to construct a society that bred the best of the best, year after year.

But to be the best, you must be ruthless.

Good leaders make sacrifices. Sometimes the sacrifices are hard, but the rewards are plentiful. Mr. Benedict made sure to indulge these leaders with their utmost desires.

A devout Catholic himself, he designed a society that rewarded his leaders with the sins that were frowned upon. If they were giving up love and happiness and joy for the betterment of the country, they deserved something in its stead.

Pride, Envy, Wrath, Sloth, Greed, Gluttony, and Lust.

Choosing leaders for this society means that it takes intense focus. Only seven are to be selected, and the investments and time are showered upon the new seven chosen every four years. The predecessors of each group of seven choose people who fit the sin that will mold them into who they are needed to be in the future—what America needs them to be. This is after a detailed study of many potential candidates. The university's acting dean behaves as a liaison for the society bringing the college applicants to the predecessors so that the selection may begin. The society members who are going out will bring forth a candidate that the society votes on and approves.

After they are chosen, the initiates are given a token and an invitation to initiation. The initiation will be a test to their character and ability to do what's right for the betterment of the society. Once the initiates pass their test, they are discreetly branded with the mark of the society, and are groomed through challenges during the course of their elite education to breed them into the influential people they were meant to be.

Once in The Elite Seven, there is no getting out. The money and power are their reward. Should they choose to stray or break the rules, the society strips them of everything. Anything they once had will be removed.

Opportunities will never arise. They will no longer have the support of the society. To this day, there have been no known occurrences of anyone from the society having to be banished. This elite group of people are what every young man and woman aspire to be a part of. While the group is a secret society, they are whispered about amongst the privileged folks in the country. Anyone who is anyone knows of the group and secretly hopes it's their son or daughter who are selected, for good fortune is showered on the family for decades to come.

VII

UINCENDUM NATUS

ENVY

VII

UINCENDUM NATUS

PROLOGUE

Sebastian

I find myself outside Sabella's house half drunk. She sleeps with the window open, and I know for a fact she leaves the front door unlocked because Sammy boy might come home late.

I hate how irresponsible you are with your privacy, my sweet girl. Anyone could come in and put their hands on you, snoop around your things, or even take them.

Makes me want to strangle Sam for leaving her to her own devices. I open the front door, then quietly close it and skim the stairs to the room I presume is hers, the pink and white curtains dancing in the wind. My heart races to find her sleeping soundly in her sleigh canopy bed—*like a princess.*

Her room is spotless. Not even a tacky Jason Momoa poster hanging above a mirror splattered with empowering girl power quotes.

There's a small vanity on the wall adjacent from her bed, and a bookshelf and desk next to the window. I skim my fingertips over her things, stopping when I come into contact with her computer.

Opening her laptop, I run my fingers over the keys, and the screen comes to life. She was last on Facebook an hour ago. I scroll to her latest post.

#Livingmybestlife.

My lips pull up into a smirk. *My troubled girl. Who are you trying to convince?*

I come to a book laying next to her computer.

Pride and Prejudice. Interesting. *I pictured you as more of a tacky romance reader.* Picking it up, I can almost feel where her hands touched it before she decided to lay down and rest her beautiful, sad eyes. My gaze drifts to her sleeping form. She's lying on her stomach, a fluffy pillow snuggled up under her head. *So cute,* yet infuriating. *Being in here and seeing the real you—the one nobody gets to see—just makes me want you more.*

Setting the book down, I step over to her vanity, picking up the half-empty perfume bottle.

Mmm…it smells of fresh laundry—*like you.* I spray it on myself to get rid of the smell of the slut I just fucked.

She stirs in her sleep, making my adrenaline spike. Setting down the bottle, I move to her bedside and pull the blankets over her back to keep the wind billowing through the cracked window from biting at her delicate skin.

"Shhh," I whisper, petting her silky hair, and she settles, my voice calming her back into a dream. *See? You do need me, you just don't know it yet.*

"Sleep, my sweet Sabella. I'll see you tomorrow."

VII

UINCENDUM NATUS

ONE

Weeks earlier
Sebastian

Twisting the eighteen-karat white gold Rolex on my wrist, I check the time. Seven forty-eight. Tick-tock, motherfucker. The evening burns August-hot, the swamp's damp life hanging from the oaks and pines with fog, making sweat bead on my skin. The smell of moss is pungent in the air, sticking to the back of my throat like mold. The sound of frogs croaking on the bank or low-lying bogs within the rotted duff of Louisiana can be heard amongst the ever growing crowd, but the adrenaline pounding in my heart becomes the soundtrack of my impending win. My hand grips the wheel of my Porsche 911 Carrera, and I turn my head to eye my opponent. Bennett Waxer. He's a beady-eyed little fucker who thinks he has it better than me. Thinks he's a better racer than me. Thinks his life is better than mine. It is, but that's temporary. When he made a remark about my car, I decided to settle the score with a race.

His spiked black hair rubs the top liner of his car, his dark eyes challenging me from across the way. He has no chance in that busted ass Mustang.

I don't pay him any mind, though. His bitch sitting in the passenger seat is why I'm doing this. Long, tan legs, hair that sweeps across her tight ass with every sway of her hips in those fucking short dresses that cling to her curves—*she* is what I'm after. She smiles, her green eyes telling me she's mine if I win. The only reason she's with that loser is because she hasn't had the chance to meet me.

Until now.

I don't want his car—I can buy twenty of those—and I don't want his sloppy clothes either.

If I'm being honest, I want a friend to slap me on the shoulder and tell me I have this, and his girl pushing the hair from my face while she tells me what she'll do to me if I win the race.

If I get her, I get everything. I mean, I have everything…but a woman at my side is something I can't lock down. They just don't seem to love me the way I need them to. They ruin everything.

"Ready?" a voice booms from my window, catching my attention. A common friend between Bennett and I. I'm friends with everybody, though. You never know who you'll need at your disposal the day the devil comes knocking for souls, and making friends with everyone gives me a goddamn army.

"Yeah." I turn my attention to the front windshield.

ENVY

A short girl in a blue jean skirt and white blouse stands in the middle of the street with her hands raised. She's on the heavier side, but it suits her. She carries those extra pounds in the right places, and she knows it.

"Ready. Set. Go!" She throws her hands down, and I stomp my foot on the pedal. My car's engine clinks and purrs under the hood just as my head slams against the headrest and we thrust forward.

With my hand on the shifter, I hit it into first, then second, followed by third. My thundering heart roars as the rhythm of the tires on burning asphalt chases adrenaline through my veins.

We're neck and neck, both of us applying a small amount of brakes as we near the blind corner. White smoke and the smell of rubber fills the air as centrifugal force takes over, nearly throwing me into the passenger seat. I sit up straight and grip the wheel at the same time I punch the gas.

The Mustang is a hair in front, but I'm not worried. I'll catch up in the straight away.

I got this.

Suddenly, Bennett's taillights shine red in the midst of my adrenaline. Why is he stopping?

Just a millisecond of confusion crosses my mind before I see why.

A truck hauling a boat suddenly backs out of the swamp, blocking the roadway. I jerk the wheel to miss Bennett, but the bite of my tires is too much for my car to handle. Rubber screams as it tears along the blacktop. I punch the brakes, and the car careens to the side, jostling my body around like a ping pong ball before running into the back of Bennett's car head on.

A kaleidoscope of colors dance in my view as metal creaks and glass pops.

Pain explodes up my leg, a sharp burning below my knee, alerting me to injury. My ears ring, the pressure in my head causing a massive headache as my crumpled vehicle lands in the swamp with a splash. Green sludge water begins to fill my car, but I have no desire to try to escape. Maybe my leg is broken, or maybe I don't want to live.

I have everything in life—riches, health, happiness—but I don't have the one thing I long for: a woman to be madly in love with me—a woman who would drop to her knees and wear a black crown marred from my family name just to be close to me. I'll whisper the terrible things I've done, and she'll love me anyway.

An explosion draws my heavy eyes to Bennett's car crumbled into the back of the trailer I forced him into when I hit him.

Warm water drifts up my face, my nose blowing bubbles, and the only thing on my mind is not getting the girl. She would have been different. She would have loved me and my flaws. I know it, and now, she's burning alive, all the pretty flesh and innocence gone.

I can hear her terrified screams as she burns, and then my head drops below the surface and her anguished cries for help sound muffled.

She's dead. I killed the girl while trying to get the girl...

VII

UINCENDUM NATUS

TWO

Laying in the hospital bed, I stare out the window, lost in a daze. The IV stuck in the crook of my arm stings. I wish there was more than saline going through it. A snort of coke would be ideal. Maybe then I wouldn't feel the stitches in my leg or the pounding of the concussion playing a goddamn orchestra in my skull. Maybe I wouldn't feel so alone. I need to numb this shit out...the emptiness. I'm usually a happy guy, seeing more than the glass half full, but my cup runneth over. I feel like God has stepped on my glass and is laughing down at me as the crimson liquid spills beneath his mighty foot.

A deep sigh vibrates my chest, and my fingers pinch the fucking ugly gown they made me wear.

The cheap, thin material irritates my skin. Flames of a Mustang flare in my vision as I look upon the blue and yellow abstract designs printed over the fabric. The sounds of screaming echoes in my ears.

Not for the first time.

But someone had to be the hero and pull me out, so here I am. Alive. Running my fingers over the IV in my arm, I wonder why I'm still hooked up. I mean, they cut the good shit hours ago. Something about being addicted wouldn't be a healthy choice for me, so now I'm on Tylenol every few hours. What a crock of shit. I just need to get out of here and self-medicate.

The familiar sound of my uncle's leather loafers tapping against the tile floor in the hallway makes my chest tighten. He's going to be pissed; he loved that car. I've always been a rebellious kid, wild and untamed. I'm the son my aunt never wanted—kids are a distraction—but life has a way of not giving a shit about what people want. When my parents were killed, my dad's brother got me, and his wife had no choice but to step up and be a mom. My uncle has a way of demanding shit, and everyone has to obey. My soul conformed to the simplicity of things rather than the hierarchy of the Westbrook name. My aunt and uncle are fatuously rich, nothing like what I was used to. My father was nothing like his brother and had been determined to keep me away from the chaotic, criminal empire my uncle ran. He found out the hard way you can't out run your past or your family. A rival enemy of my uncle's found his concealed little secret. *Us*. I was hidden in a closet when they came through our house like a tornado, executing my father before they took turns raping my mother to death. Shit like that can change a person, especially a kid. I guess I got lucky; I turned out normal. My uncle avenged my parents and took care of me out of guilt more than anything.

The only time they show up in my life is to fix shit I break or buy me stuff to replace love. Our family comes from a long line of criminal inheritance. Pushing drugs across borders, amongst other things they dip their fingers in. *"This life isn't one you'd fit into, Sebastian. You're erratic and always seeking approval. It's unbecoming—and not what the Westbrook name is built on. You're too like your father."*

Fuck him and his "life." I don't need him or his legacy. I'll make my own. My wife and children will come from a line of something earned rather than handed down.

The smell of cigar smoke and heavy spice wafts into the room before my uncle even steps in. He appears in the doorway, an unlit cigar drooping from his pale lips. I'm surprised he's not smoking, telling everyone who passes to fuck off. He's wearing an expensive suit, as usual. His hairline is fading with age, giving way to his wrinkled forehead. The room's temperature takes a dip as he nears. I know I've been pushing my luck lately.

He leans on the cane passed down to him by his father. Just looking at the intricate carvings and distress withering the bottom makes my skin burn. I've lost count of how many times I've seen him crack it over people's backs before. He's not shy when it comes to punishing the weak or traitors.

"Sebastian." My name slips past his lips like a curse. I'm not surprised, though. I live life to the fullest with a smile on my face. Sometimes, that involves breaking rules, which is usually followed by repercussions that lay upon my family who are not pleased with the unwanted attention I bring.

"Sir, visiting hours—"

"That will be all!" He dismisses the nurse hovering behind him—the one who's been assigned to me—with a cutthroat tone. Her eyes flick to mine with concern, and I slightly nod. She's older, but by the way she holds herself, she's timid. Head hung low, eyes never making contact. My uncle would eat her like a gazelle if she tried to argue with him.

He steps to the side, closing the door behind him before hitting me with cobra sharp eyes.

"Sloppy, Sebastian." His jaw tightens with tension as he speaks his authority.

Rubbing the back of my neck, I look up at the ceiling. I'd do anything for some real painkillers right now.

"It was an accident. What do you want me to say?" I huff, irritated.

It's not like I meant to wreck my car. I loved that thing.

"Bullshit. You totaled a car and two lives are gone because of your reckless behavior! Now, I'm up shit creek kissing the asses of two families while praying to God they don't try to sue us!"

Fucking liar! No one would ever get that far. He'd rather bury their entire family than risk the courts. The smirk forming on his lips gives his lie away.

"Let them. He was an adult. He knew what he was doing just as much as the tart in the passenger seat." My tone is deriding. My mind sets on the girl I could have had. I can't remember her name, but it's not important. Oh, the fun we could have had. She seemed up for adventure. I liked that about her. I need a woman down to ride the rollercoaster of my spur-of-the-moment life.

"Don't be so gauche." His nostrils flare, his dark eyes

stabbing into me with disdain. "Your fascination with playing pointless games with people's lives to better your own is over!"

Ha. Like he can fucking talk. Hypocrite.

Growing up, I always wondered how other people lived. What TV shows they watched, what kind of plates they ate off. Did they have a bedtime, did their parents argue?

It all started when I was a kid. Walking home after school, kids would follow me on their bikes and laugh, because not only did I not own a bicycle, I was seconds away from busting out of my hand-me down shoes and Flintstone-ing it home. I remember passing house after house, wondering what it would be like to be someone else. We were dirt fucking poor when I was a kid. My dad had always happy to work shit jobs and live a simple life because he was too proud to have anything to do with my uncle's criminal life.

Until, one night, it all came crashing down. I went from having shit to having everything. I've wanted for nothing since my uncle and aunt took me in. Still, I continue to stay fixated on what it's like to be someone else in this lifetime. To have a girlfriend who's too clingy, a family who laughs and invites you over for Sunday dinner—everything I don't have.

My uncle and aunt weren't built to be parents. I was raised by the men who worked for him and their women. Don't get me wrong, I loved being around them all, but I was always kept at an arm's length. No one really loved me like I needed. Hell, I don't think they even know how to love. To them, raising a boy was to make him a man as fast as possible. By the time I was of age, I had mastered the skill of fucking. I was told to show no emotion and have only two things on my mind: success and power.

All I know is I'll never be that dirty poor kid again, but I'll never be their kid either.

His cane stabs into the tile as he comes to my bedside.

"I think this built-up energy of yours can be put to better use."

"Is that so?" I pull at the stupid scratchy cotton gown making me hot. Why am I even in here still? I'm fucking fine.

"Yes." The tone in his voice conveys an underlying tale, and my eyes snap to his.

"Your aunt wants you to go to college. She thinks it will be good for you."

I roll my eyes, holding back my scoff. She just wants me out the house, out of her hair.

"Sebastian, this can work in our favor. The family's favor."

Curiosity has me interested in hearing him out. "What do you have in mind?"

"You will prove yourself useful to me. Up until now, you've been allowed your…playtime."

Playtime?

"But it's time for you to use your potential, earn your place in *my* world." He waves his hand through the air, as if he's literally showing me his kingdom, before waltzing to the other side of the room to look out the window. I snap upright in the bed.

"What is it you actually want from me, to just go to school and what, be a good student?" I scoff. How can he want that? How will that do anything but get me out the way? I'm his fucking blood.

ENVY

He turns, pointing his finger at me.

"I'm serious about this. You will do your part for the Westbrook name. Our name must strive. I will not allow anything else while I'm walking this earth!"

I know I haven't been the ideal *son*. Everywhere I turn, I seem to step into trouble, whether I intend to or not. I am the fucking poster boy for a bad presence, but I can't help it. Seeing someone with something better than me boils my blood. I will not rest until I've shown I'm more commendable. That people admire me. What can I say? I perform like I never lose. Me carrying the Westbrook name will only strengthen it.

"What do you want from me?" My tone is softer. My gut spirals as tight as a corkscrew, knowing he wants something and I'll have to go through with whatever it is. I have no one else, and he knows that. It's almost as if he did this on purpose, letting me ride all these years to now turn around and cash in the many luxuries I've been afforded. Nowhere to run. You can't expect loyalty from those who starve for money.

"I want you to go to one of the best schools there is." He smirks.

"What do you want me to do, mule drugs to the rich kids?" Westbrooks don't supply to normal civilians, only celebrities or those in politics. He could bury just about any A-lister if he wanted.

He laughs, looking up at the ceiling with mockery in his eyes. He would trust me with drugs just about as much as he would trust a toddler detailing his new Bentley.

"Why don't you just show me how to run the damn business!" My tone rises, and he still chuckles to himself. I've asked repeatedly for him to teach me the ropes, and every time, he shuts me down. What does he want from me?

"Oh, boy, Westbrooks own the empire. We don't do fool's work. I have something else in mind for you." His eyes fall to mine, and his tone intrigues me. I can do anything he can, and he knows it. He's afraid to let me in. He knows I'm fucking smart and could put him out on his ass if I wanted to. He doesn't trust me. There's no trust in this family. Never has been. Never will be. Never can be. It's just the nature of the business.

"What then?" I grind out. I'll prove to him how fucking skilled I am.

"Your aunt wants you to go to college, and I have the perfect one for you."

"It's too late to join college. Classes already started," I say, matter of fact. He just needs to cut the shit and tell me where he wants me. Wherever it is, I'll do it. I'll surmount any task he gives me because I'm worthy of his trust, of anything he thinks I can do, to show him I'm not a kid anymore.

"We pulled some strings, Sebastian. Your grades have always been well above that of your peers, and your skills with a computer speak for themselves. Add a little cash donation, and I secured you a place at none other than St. Augustine."

Of course he did. Jesus Christ.

"Sounds to me like you just want me out of the picture."

Of course he would recommend school even though nobody in my family has gone to college, not even him. Hell, half the outlaws working for us never even finished high school. We learn everything from the streets and first-hand experience.

"You know me better than that, Sebastian. I've always allowed you to carve your own path, but now it's time to payback everything your aunt and I have given you."

"So, you just want me to go to college?" I ask, nonchalant.

"St. Augustine isn't just a college, it's something much bigger," he forewarns, conveying this isn't going to be four years of partying. Dropping my hands on either side of me, I tilt my head to the side, observing my uncle with unforgiving eyes.

"I know what it is—the campus made of urban legends. That's your big plan?" St. Augustine is supposedly the hardest college to get into in the south because of a rumored secret society. Might as well rub a fucking lamp and see if a genie pops out.

A brief grin tugs up his lips, and his eyes fucking sparkle with delight.

"Oh, it's not a myth. The Elite Seven is very real. Only seven candidates are chosen, and if they prove worthy, they're given everything their heart desires. Their influence is beyond anything money has ever bought me."

"What are you saying? You want me to find out who is in this society?"

"I want you to get in, to be one of those seven candidates."

Is he fucking high? *Probably.*

"How?" I ask, intrigued by the idea of being part of something bigger than myself—something outside of my fucked-up life and the Westbrook name.

"That's for you to figure out. And, Sebastian?" He says my name with an intense edge. "This is your chance to prove yourself to me. I know you can do this. Get yourself into The Elite so we can call upon them shall we ever need to." He turns, the sound of his cane causing goosebumps to race along my spine.

I would need a degree in something. The only thing I could see myself doing is something with computers. It's crazy the shit you can do with the right computer. The things you can find. Nothing is safe on the dark web. I fucking love it. I'm always creeping behind the clueless eyes on the other side of the screen. This is what's going to give me an edge, a way to infiltrate this Elite and get in. I'll prove I'm more than fucking worthy of the life he granted me and the trust he's giving me. With a group as powerful as The Elite, I'll be able to have anything I want and make the world quiver beneath me.

But what business do I have at a fucking school? What the hell kind of business do I have strutting around a campus?

The idea of a school, books, and homework makes me more vengeful by the thought.

But then, a brief glimpse of women wearing skirts, flipping their flower-smelling hair over their shoulders, and looking at me with fuck-me eyes has me grinning with temptation. My cup runneth over, motherfucker.

If I do this right, I could have everything I've ever wanted—everyone would want to be me.

THREE

My fingertips tap the slacks forming to my thighs, my handmade Burluti's shoes patting the floorboard to the hum of the tires on the smooth asphalt. Looking out the limo's window, the grounds of the college take on a Greek appearance. White stone bricks stand as high as the eye can see with pillars reminding me of something out of a mythology book. The shrubs and greenery vining up the walls makes me feel like Zeus, not some guy with a troubled past forced into an education as a last resort.

This is far from the private school I attended as a teenager—a place people paid top dollar just to say their kid went to Newton Academy.

No, this place is the real deal.

The limo comes to a stop, the vehicle gently rocking

as our driver climbs out and opens my door. The light from the sun blinds me. I raise my hand, blocking its harsh rays as I step out. I straighten my shirt, my eyes looming across the grounds.

It's stunning. Trees billow over couples sitting on benches. A woman blushes as her partner raises his hand up her skirt. My teeth bite into my bottom lip, my slacks getting tighter as my dick grows behind the zipper.

I can have that. I need that. I'll get that.

"Mr. Westbrook?" The driver wrestles my bags from the trunk, then stands there puffing out air as he looks at me expectantly. My hair falls in my eyes as I turn my attention to him. His gray, flossy hair is parted over his head, trying to cover up the baldness, and his scrawny frame conveys he doesn't have much more time on this earth. "Good luck. Mr. Westbrook said he put enough money in your account to get you through the semester. If you need anything, call upon your uncle." He slams the hood and weakly walks back to the driver side, making sure to keep one hand on the car to steady himself.

Good luck? What does he mean? Isn't he going to take my bags up? My uncle thought it best I stay on campus, in the thick of it all, right in the sights of The Elite. More like he doesn't trust me not to go find trouble to get into off campus, so looks like I'm dorming it. What a fucking joke. I glance around for a bellboy or someone to greet my arrival, but everyone walks around me, nobody stopping to help me carry my things or direct me to where the fuck I should be going.

I really am on my own.

Turning the watch on my wrist, I glance around the common grounds. People smile and nod in my direction.

ENVY

They don't even know me, yet they're acting as if we're best fucking buds. I like it.

"Hey, take one!" Some tall, preppy-looking fucker with no facial hair grins at me before shoving a flier in my arms.

Taking the yellow piece of paper, I look it over. It's some initiation to join a frat house.

Before I'm done reading it, more and more fliers are pounded into my hands. Parties, invitations, groupies.

"Oh, take this!" Some guy who looks as if he should be predicting the weather tries to hand me a piece of paper, and I glare at him. My jaw tightens, my shoulders rising, daring him. He stops, his hand mid-air. Standing silently, he looks away, gulps, then steps back.

Jesus, I mean, I'm all for friendly, but give me a fucking break.

Placing the papers in my teeth, I grab my bags off the ground and look for the main office. My uncle pulled strings to get me in here, and upon my arrival, I'm supposed to check in with some academic counselor named Mrs. Griffin.

I did my homework after I left the hospital, my uncle's words turning in my head nonstop. I learned everything about this town, the people in it, the power players, and the ones most likely to be part of this Elite society. Candidates come from this school, so someone must be pulling the strings from within, hence my meeting with the ever-so-lovely Mrs. Griffin. Counselor of the school, wife of the dean, and sister to one of the most influential men in this town, a Mr. Benedict the Third. His name appears in nearly every shareholder documents for this town, and his family name is linked to every whisper of

The Elite over the years. He's a string puller, and Mrs. Griffin is attached to them, I just know it.

Also while I'm there, I'll get my schedule and figure out more about the woman and just how thick she's in with things here.

I debate finding out where I'm rooming first, but curiosity gets the better of me and I head toward the main building.

Walking across the concrete path, I can't help but notice all the couples, blissfully happy together. They don't need anything else because they have each other. The way the women sway into their significant others with need and affection. The possessive expressions on the men's faces as they look at their girls with idolization. How come I can't have that? Is it because I know exactly what I want? Am I too demanding? Maybe, if I just let loose like them, I could be happy.

My chest burns. My fingers tingle. I have to close my eyes to settle my rapid heartbeat. I hate this feeling—this jealous strike of abandonment that thuds deep in my soul. Thoughts of murdering the males and their women always comes next.

Like that couple. He's taller than her, wearing some stupid ass sweater, even though it's hot as fuck outside, and his hair is styled taller than a southern woman in church. I could take him out and slide right up to his blonde bombshell of a girlfriend without so much as breaking a sweat. I could be good to her, as long as she loved me as much. We could have fun. She'd never miss him.

That killing seems so easy scares me sometimes. Maybe it's wired into my DNA. My uncle didn't get where he is without hiding a few bodies.

ENVY

Inside the building, I glance left, then right, before finding the office floor numbers.

Sighing, I reign in the hounds of my worst mental habits and focus on settling in to my new playground.

Counselor. Ground floor. Getting a better handle on my bags, I head around the corridors. People walk in groups, everyone already settling in and finding their place. They're so consumed with each other, they don't look where they're going. One dude bumps into me, nearly knocking the million leaflets out of my hand.

"Dude!" I frown. He turns abruptly with narrowed eyes, but his attitude soon changes when he sees my posture.

Fucking say something, dick. I dare you. I scowl.

I throw my flyers at him, and he blinks rapidly before turning away. I run my hand through my hair in an attempt to calm myself. Fucking people and their attitudes. Why couldn't he just apologize?

Passing door after door, the scent of paper, highlighter ink, and coffee becomes thick in the air as I come across a small room with an ink-haired vixen slapping the shit out of her computer monitor. It's comical, really. Small, but feisty.

Nibbling on my lip, I take her in, smiling at how fucking easy this makes my life.

Her hair is black as night, matching her cat-like eyes. Her body is sleek, perfect. I can't help but wonder if she could be the one—the one I want to make mine. She's so much younger than any counselor I've seen. Not saying I've seen a lot, but still. Her pictures on the net don't do her justice.

Slumping in her chair, her eyes flick to mine before

doing a double take.

"Come in!" She positions her screen to where it's centered on her desk, trying to rein herself in.

Stepping inside her office, the smell of cinnamon and something spicy swirls around me like a storm in the middle of monsoon season. The room is filled with minimal décor, a big ass filing cabinet hugging most of one wall.

"What's wrong with it?" I try to act casual, gesturing to her computer as I slightly lift the corner of my lips in that way girls like.

"Trying to pull up a file and it just keeps freezing," she huffs, agitated.

"Let me take a look for you." Without waiting for permission, I reach over and start typing on the frozen screen.

She frowns, but moves away to stand on the other side of her desk as she watches me work.

"You have a virus," I inform her right off the bat. It's not a lie. I sent it to her this morning in the form of an email. I knew who she was and planned my attack accordingly. If I'm going to get into The Elite, knowing every fucked-up backstory of the people involved is one way to start. Her being the dean's wife, she has to have dirty little secrets.

"What? How?" She folds her slender arms over her chest, pushing her tits up, until the mounds peek out the top of her blouse. *Tease.*

I take that rhetorically as I lose myself in the task of adding a sharing app and hiding it within her data so she'll never know I'm able to see and access everything she does from the luxury of my laptop. This is too easy.

"You really know what you're doing, don't you?" She seems impressed, and the flirty inflection in her tone doesn't go unnoticed.

Oh, Mrs. Griffin, you're going to be fun to play with.

I smile and keep at what I'm doing.

"I'm going to install a better firewall. It's a free one, so it will only hold up for so long, but it should keep peeping toms away from your personal information."

I look over my shoulder at her, unable to help myself. "Unless you like peeping toms?" I flirt back, my eyes roaming across her creamy collarbone.

After I'm done installing what I need, I grab the apple off her desk and sink my teeth into it. Her eyes narrow at my brashness, but if she intended to eat it, she would have, right?

Popping my ass on the corner of her desk, I chew the apple, staring at her. Ironic, isn't it? I'm eating the forbidden fruit of biblical times and fairy tales while ogling a married woman as if she's my next meal.

Placing herself behind her desk, she can't help but glance at me, trying to decide if she likes me. I wink at her. Things could get interesting if she'd like.

She doesn't bite. Her eyes flick back to her computer.

"You should really stay off the porn," I say around a mouthful of apple.

"I—" she starts, attempting to defend herself, but when my eyes shoot to hers, she clicks out of the screen quickly.

Dirty girl. I see everything. In fact, I see her without even having to dig into her secrets. Her tight dress and heavy makeup. She wants to be seen, but the glint in her eyes says she's angry too. Carrying a vendetta of sorts. Maybe against a man, or perhaps all mankind. Walking around like she's good enough to eat just so she can turn us down. Cock tease.

She clicks on her computer, squinting her eyes, then sits back, folding her arms and studying me.

"I like porn. Sex is a healthy way to release tension," she tells me, making my mouth drop open.

"Now, thank you for your help, but I'm expecting a student any minute." Her cutthroat tone makes me swallow. Who could she desperately want to see over me? I just helped her clear her computer of evidence pointing to the slut she is—albeit that's not all I did. Deep throating cock while being bound. I wonder what her superiors would say if I'd left that on her desktop.

"Like who?"

My picture flickers on her screen.

"Hmm…" She glances up at me. "Sebastian Westbrook?"

Sliding off her desk, I drop my ass in the chair and grin. Maybe I'm not the only one who's done their research. She has an entire file on me. I rub my neck, suddenly feeling anxious. She knows more about me than I'd like, thanks to my fucking parents' death making the headlines all those years back.

"I'm Mrs. Griffin," she says, formally introducing herself.

Oh, I know who you are, sweetness.

"Dean's daughter?" I ask, just to watch the flush of her skin. Women love compliments.

I already know she's not the sweet dean's daughter. That little blonde beauty is nothing like the woman standing before me now. Now, *Chastity* would be a challenge—one I'd take up in a heartbeat. I'd beat her pussy until it was so stretched out, Daddy would have to pay for plastic surgery.

Her lips purse, a vindictive sneer crossing her face. "Mmm...cute." She's not buying my charm. "Moving on, Sebastian. I can promise you nothing we say will be repeated. What we share in here is just between us two. I only want the best for you." She's a shitty liar. She'll tell my secrets to whomever will listen. I can tell just by looking at her.

"I can help you succeed here, if you prove willing," she adds.

My head tilts to the side as I take in her robotic tone.

"I'm willing," I reply. I want what's best for me too. Maybe it's her. My desperation for companionship is deafening. All brought back to being starved of affection as a child. I used to sneak into my uncle and aunt's room every now again to watch them fuck. My uncle is a rough man, hands wrapped around my aunt's shoulders like a coiled snake bounding his prey. But she wasn't the only pussy he entertained in that room. One time, I saw him with a woman much younger than him, and I'll never forget the one stray rose clinched between her teeth. She couldn't yell because the thorns would prick her if she dared to move her lips. The look in her eyes didn't convey she was hurting or scared, but they didn't gloss with the feeling of being cherished either. She looked...hypnotized. My uncle's eyes glistened with power and strength. I've never seen him look so...in control before.

My mind fleets back to the moment I asked him about his infidelity

"Why did that woman have a rose in her mouth?" It's the question that's been lingering in my mind for days.

My uncle's eyes snap over the paper he's reading, boring

into mine.

He swallows, setting his newspaper down.

"It conveys something you cannot say, but feel." His tone is low, and there's anger in his eyes.

Eating my eggs benedict, I wonder what that something might be. I've always thought a rose is just that—a flower.

"Sometimes ultimate power comes from the dominance over the body of another."

I nod, and think back to the crimson color of a rose biting into the delicate lips of a sinner.

I want that look—the look of deranged love. That kind of love is what I need.

"Talk to me. Tell me something about you." Mrs. Griffin's voice takes me out of the memory, and I instantly want to hurt her. You know the feeling. Like when you see a small child and you want to smile and hug them, but you can't help that deep, irrational feeling of snatching up their sticky little hand and squeezing it until they cry for you to let go? When I don't answer, she continues.

"For example, where is your head coming into all… this?" she huffs, tapping her fingernail on her desk. *This? As in school?*

She doesn't give a shit. She's bored, and so am I.

"What do you want me to say?" I growl in response. I'm not an angry person, but talking about *feelings* is not my idea of fun. To feel things as deeply and personal as I do is a curse.

"I read in your file that you just witnessed a couple of your peers burning alive in a car. How did that make you feel?"

What a cliché fucking question. How did it make me feel? It made me feel…

"Like the devil," I confess. Her dark brows furrow, but there's a twitch in her lips like she wants to smile.

"I wanted something I couldn't have, so it was only natural nobody should have it," I explain further. Bennet didn't deserve the life he had.

"Interesting. I don't believe you're the devil, Sebastian." She moves some papers around her desk, but doesn't make eye contact. She's lying. If she's seen all the things I'm capable of, she'd be singing a different tune.

"Aren't I, though? Why else would I be single and so fucking…" I pause, the idea of saying I'm lonely making me feel weak.

"You don't feel like you're worthy?" Her forehead tries to wrinkle as she attempts to piece together my life in the short time we've been in each other's presence.

"Let's just say there is the man I am, and the one I wish I was."

"Well, even the devil was loved. He was God's beloved son and chose to rebel. Maybe that's what you're doing." She smirks now, her eyes ignited with intrigue.

"Maybe." I shrug. "Or maybe I want to be beloved again."

When silence cloaks the room, her face takes on a bored look, as if she's grown tired of my replies. That's funny. I thought she was supposed to tell me how to walk the line and step into the fucking sunlight.

She clears her throat.

"I feel like that's enough for today. Here is where you will take up residence for the duration of your stay." She hands me a map with a room circled in red pen. I sigh. I'm not excited about staying in a fucking dorm. She taps her nail against her desk, her eyes elsewhere. An awkwardness settles between us, indicating I've overstayed my welcome. Thank God.

Standing, I give her a curt nod and grab my things.

"Um, Sebastian?"

I flick my gaze to hers, her cat-like eyes shining with temptation.

"Thank you for your help with my computer. And just so you're aware, your talents have been noticed today. I think you could be a good fit within St. Augustine, depending on your plans to be either the king of the sinners himself or the good guy, of course."

"I'll keep that in mind."

"My door is open if there's anything you need to help you decide."

Anything? She's offering more than a chat. I knew she wanted me. This bitch knows her way around a man, and I find it very intriguing. I'm almost envious of the dean. I bet his nights are never dull with this hell cat. Was she dropping hints about The Elite with her sinner comment? Damn, I'm intrigued.

I continue out the door without looking back.

The bitch wouldn't know what being good is if it smacked her in the face.

VII

UINCENDUM NATUS

FOUR

The dorms are close to the main campus. The one I'm assigned is about four stories high, made from the same white stone brick as the rest of the structures. Vibrant flyers plaster the glass doors leading into the building. When someone steps out of the door, the overwhelming smell of popcorn and pizza almost knocks me off my feet.

I have every thought in mind to call my uncle and demand I stay somewhere more reasonable, but I am not about to bow down and admit I need his help and money already. I'm Sebastian Westbrook. I can do this.

If anything, this is probably a test to see if I can withstand a challenge.

Grabbing the door before it shuts, I shuffle my bags inside and notice a directory on the wall right in front of me. I'm on the second floor. Throwing my bag over my shoulder, I stomp up the steps. A couple students pass by, giving me awkward eyes, and I greet them back with a Joker-worthy smile.

A chick with pigtails and a sucker in the corner of her mouth takes the bait, smiling flirtatiously.

Nipping at my bottom lip, I watch her walk away. Tight ass. Thick thighs. I'd fuck her from behind just to watch that ass bounce.

Finally making it to the second fucking floor, I adjust my bags over my shoulder and search for room D-twelve. Arrows just above the stairwell tell me where the D rooms are. Left.

People stand in the halls, chatting outside their rooms. Some are sprawled out on the floor sharing popcorn and talking over textbooks, and some are tossing clothes back and forth between rooms. The white fabric flies through the air as if it's lost and being carried by the wind.

This is a fucking circus. I'll never survive here. I went from maids and butlers to this.

Finally reaching D-twelve, I find the door open. There are two small beds on each side of the room. The one on the right is clearly my roommate's. It's already made with what looks like some Star Wars blankets or some shit. Posters of comics and articles are plastered along the wall, and a metal desk teetering on a Tylenol bottle to even it out sits just behind the bed. The top of the desk is full of figurines, an old looking laptop, and a black flashy camera.

My eyes fall to what I assume is my side. It's bland, dull. The bed has one gray blanket and a white pillow. The desk seems level at least. Flicking my eyes around the room, I find a small closet. Just one. They want us to share.

This isn't going to do. I need privacy.

"Excuse me! Excuse me!" A whiny voice scratches into the air before I'm practically shoved out of the way. A short male wearing slacks and a white button-up shirt hustles by me. His hair is dark and unruly, curling around his white-framed glasses.

He sits down at his desk, placing a cup near the far side of the desk, and begins typing away. So, this is my roommate. I crack my neck, awkward silence filling the air.

He isn't going to tell me his name? Say hello? Fucking acknowledge me at the very least?

My brows pinch together, unsure of this unusual fellow. He's clearly a mouth breather by the sound of that heavy wheezing. Great, he'll be a blast to sleep next to.

I close the door behind me and stride up beside him. I look over his shoulder to see what has his attention. He's lost in code flashing across his screen. His eyes widen as he murmurs something to himself and jots it down on a notepad.

I grab his cup off his desk, and his attention snaps to me.

I sniff it. Smells like some kind of fucking tea.

"Hey!" he shouts.

Raising a brow, I take a sip, the warm herbal remedy filling my mouth. Swallowing the piss, I make a hissing sound as it slips down my throat.

"Name's Sebastian," I introduce myself.

He blinks a few times, taking me in. This is supposed to be a school full of money and brains, and this guy seems to be short on both. I've seen men in Gucci suits and chicks with the most expensive heels strut by, and then there's this cat. He's definitely not what I was expecting.

Setting his cup back down, I point to it.

"That could use some whiskey. Tastes like shit." He doesn't respond. Using his index finger, he pushes his glasses closer to his face and continues to stare me over.

I flop down on his bed to make sure it's not better than mine. The springs screech trying to withstand my weight. The blankets smell new.

"I'm Oliver Olly."

Olly. I know that name. His father is some big news reporter for CGN or some shit. I bet that's how he got in here.

I sit up, my legs moving to the floor. I'd take a bare room over Olly's shit.

Standing, I head over to my bed and rest on my back, my arms behind my head. I can feel him staring at me, the beam of geek practically rubbing off on me.

"I like to work in silence. I'm not a party person and like lights out by ten," he mumbles.

My face scrunches, and I look over to him.

"Yeah, that shit isn't going to work for me. You're going to have to find another room."

"What?" His voice takes on a higher pitch. "We're assigned our rooms." He frowns.

He gets up, opens the door, and hurries over to his laptop. "I like the door open."

"Oily," I bark, making him startle.

"It's Olly," he offers meekly.

I grab out my own laptop and flip it open, my hands flitting over the keys, breaking down the firewalls for the school's computer files and finding housing. There are always rooms put to the side for exchanges and late comers. Olly just got a new roommate. Getting to my feet and yanking his laptop from the desk, I place my own there. "See? You're in D-eighteen with a lovely guy named Buddy."

"My paperwork said D-twelve." He looks completely dumbfounded. Fucking hell, just leave already.

"Printing error." I shrug. "Shut the door on your way out. I like it closed." I smirk.

Knowing he's not going to win this battle, he snatches his shit up and rambles on about how the office admin could make such a stupid error. Meanwhile, questions about The Elite buzz around my head. Everyone here is loaded with riches and power, so why the fuck is joining this club so great?

Mind you, if I were one of the seven, I wouldn't need my uncle or his money anymore. I'd have a brotherhood to turn to. I would be rich and could do what I want without having to worry about who I embarrass.

Olly scoffs and starts shoving his shit into a black bag.

If they do exist, what would my heart desire the most? That's easy: a woman.

I'll be the big bad wolf and she'll be dressed in red, falling to her knees while offering me her forbidden apple.

I wonder when we'll know who got picked for the secret society. Going back to my laptop, I decide to do a little digging into Mrs. Griffin's computer.

Sins and sacrifice were the main words I found to describe the secret society when I did an intense search about them, but no details on how to be chosen. Maybe I just need to stand out amongst the students here, show whomever is in charge of this Elite I'm worthy. Twisting my watch, I wonder how I could do that without drawing too much attention to myself and getting kicked out.

Clicking into Lillian's files, I dig deep, go where nobody wants anyone to find anything. Usually, people will put it under a file with a stupid name hoping nobody will have the curiosity to look any further.

A password box flashes up on the screen. Only those with something to hide need extra password protection. I bypass it and find a file with a skull and crown on it. It's by itself on a black screen desktop.

I click it.

There are seven names, with seven sins.

This must be the chosen for The Elite. Mrs. Griffin must have something to do with the chosen. I fucking knew that bitch was in this deep.

Biting my lip, I look the list over.

Mason Blackwell—Pride.

Samuel Gunner—Wrath.

Rhett Masters—Lust.

Rush Dempsey—Sloth.

Micah Dixon—Greed.

Baxter Samuel Goddard the Fifth—Gluttony.

Oliver Olly—Envy.

No fucking way. My eyes track Olly packing up his shit. This fucking guy? My chest constricts knowing the seven have already been chosen and I'm not on the list. I need to be on this fucking list. It's my only chance at triumphing over my uncle, proving to him I'm worthy of everything he's given me.

Chewing on my lip, I glare at the chosen seven. I could just put myself on the list.

ENVY

Raising a brow, I slip the cursor toward the bottom sinner's name, delete Oliver Olly, and type Sebastian Westbrook in its place, every press of the key syncing to the rhythm of my heart. I smirk over at the loser in the room.

"Sorry, Olly boy, but The Elite is no place for a geek like you. Consider me doing you a favor."

Sitting back, I look at my name.

Sebastian Westbrook—Envy

It looks like it belongs on that list.

This is it. I'm going to get everything I wanted. My uncle will be proud at how fast I infiltrated The Elite.

My stomach growls, and it occurs to me I haven't eaten today.

"What's to eat around here?" I ask Oliver before he flees the room.

"Mmm, they serve dinner at certain times in the main hall. There's a sitting room on the main floor with a microwave if you brought your own food," he informs. He moves over to his bed and squats to his knees. That's when I notice food items stashed in a little clear tub toward the back. Microwavable mac and cheese, Ramen noodles, popcorn, and a few bottles of water—shit I used to eat when I was a poor kid.

"I'll eat out." I grimace, the thought of a burger or something greasy sounding more appetizing.

"Suit yourself," he murmurs, grabbing the tub from under the bed.

"Can you help me move my stuff to the right room?" he asks, and I wince.

"Sorry, Oily, I need to go get some food. I'm starving."

I grab my jacket and waltz past him.

"It's Olly," he calls after my retreating form.

I push out into the brisk air and inhale. This place is beyond busy, and I'm not used to being around so many people. I bring up a map of the surrounding area on my phone to find somewhere to get food, but get distracted by none other than Mrs. Griffin. She strides up to a slick black car. A two-thousand-and-sixteen Mercedes Benz CLS four-hundred. I know my cars, and that's one nice fucking vehicle for an academic counselor. She not flying under the radar, that's for sure. Her heels click against the concrete as she slips in behind the wheel and starts it. The car purrs to life. She attempts to pull out of the space, but stops. Getting out, she throws her hands up and starts to pace. Something is wrong.

I move closer without thought and take in her distress. It makes me want to do things to her. Her cat-like eyes crawl across me like a huntress, making me squirm. "I have a flat," she huffs, shaking her head.

"Mrs. Griffin." I smile, looking around her. Moving closer, I see the slice in the tire. It's not just a flat; it's a deliberate puncture. She must not be liked around here.

"You may call me Lillian." She smiles tightly.

Oh, I know your name, babe.

Silence settles between us, and I can't help but wonder how far she lives from campus. Is the dean waiting on her for dinner? Does she cook? What's her life like?

"I'm going to walk and have someone tow it." She breaks the silence.

"Sounds wise." I smile.

"How are you settling in? Have you met your new roommate?" Her counselor tone takes over, and I grit my teeth. Is this really how every conversation with her is going to be? Did she put me with Olly on purpose? Is this all a test? It must be. There's no way Olly would be on that list over me.

"Fine," is all I say.

Her cell begins to ring, and her eyes widen in relief. "I have to get this. Let me know how you settle in, Sebastian." She smirks, her cat eyes sending a shiver down my spine, then turns on her heel to begin her walk home.

She's different. She radiates the same evil aura as me. My hands rub together in anticipation. She's going to be fun. A woman I could play with before I completely devoured her mentally.

I want to know more about her. What does her house look like? Her bed? Is she a cat or dog person? I leave thoughts of food behind and decide to find out.

Waiting a few beats for her to gain ground, I follow her. I'm only a block behind her, staring at her tight ass flexing with each stiletto strut. She can't see me. Peeking around each building, my body becomes one with the shadows. I'd give Michael Myers a run for his money in the stalking territory. Man, I hate that word. It's just intense curiosity.

Rounding another block just behind Lillian, I hear her ringtone sound out. Some kind of pop music. She's oblivious she's being watched. Most women are.

Such a naughty girl. You shouldn't be on your phone so distracted, Mrs. Griffin. It's not safe.

Her footfalls slow, and my feet sigh in relief. Her house is two stories, nice looking. Seems more suited for a "Leave It To Beaver" family than a little vixen like herself. I know records will show it's the husband on the deed, not her. It's a reddish color with a trellis climbing up the sides and bushes perfectly placed just out front.

She mounts the few steps to her door. Sliding my hands in my pocket, I step behind a tree and watch her. The night is silent, the wind steady as I focus solely on her. The lights flick on inside, her shadow passing along the wall before she steps in front of what I assume is the living room windows. Reaching behind her back, satisfaction crosses her features just before her hand pulls a black bra free of her top, her breasts falling slightly from the weight.

"Yeah. That's better, isn't it?" I whisper into the night. I can imagine what her nipples look like. Big pink areoles and little rose-colored nips.

I can't control the smirk flitting across my face. Watching her without her knowing is a thrill. Headlights rise just above the passing hill, and I slide up against the tree, hoping not to be seen. A car pulls into the driveway. It's the dean. It's so dark, I can't see much of him from here, but I can tell it's him. Medium build, grayish hair. He unworthy of a woman like Lillian.

Jealousy runs through my veins. He'll get to see Mrs. Griffin's perky nipples tonight, eat pizza with her, and have her at his side at bedtime. He doesn't know what to do with a woman of her magnitude.

Inhaling, I twist the watch on my wrist, irritated. I could gaze upon Lillian all night if it weren't for him. Watch her bathe and clean herself. Watch TV and laugh at some stupid sitcom. Fucking dean.

It's getting late, and I have a long walk back home.

"Another time, Lillian. Another time."

Glaring at the dean's shadow, I turn and stomp back to my fucking dorm. Alone.

VII

UINCENDUM NATUS

FIVE

Heading into my first class of the day, the room smells of dry eraser and coffee. I'm not late, but I'm not early either. I've seen some familiar faces around campus, and one I know to be on the list of Elite candidates is Samuel Gunner. He's some badass fighter according to a Facebook group, and if I did my research right, which I did, we have class together today, along with one other brother. I ran into Samuel on campus before class one day. Our conversation was short-lived, but informative. I need in deeper. Befriending The Elite is my first priority today.

I have to shift through legs and bags just to find an empty spot damn near the middle of the fucking room. Dropping my shit on the floor, I slide into my desk, slouch back, and people watch—what I do best. It's interesting the things you notice and hear when strangers are oblivious to wandering eyes and ears. My eyes snap straight forward to a couple a few rows in front of me. Rhett Masters. His picture is all over the internet. Dubbed Lust on the list, and Romeo by his high school classmates. A few rows from him is Samuel Gunner. Wrath. He comes from a wealthy family and is known in the underground fighting circuit. He doesn't look as roguish in his normal clothes compared to the images of him online. Rubbing my chin, I watch them, curious if they are any different than me.

They are both dressed down in comparison. Samuel's face is contorted in anger—daddy or mommy issues I would assume—and Rhett seems broken. The creases in his forehead foreshadow something much darker within him. A couple next to Rhett grabs my attention when the girl leans into the guy intimately, her honey brown hair hiding half her face. The shmuck has an arrogant look smeared across his face as he cups her cheek. I stand and shuffle back through the seated students, making a scene. Just as I find the empty seat next to her, I drop into it and lean back, chewing on the end of my pencil. I can feel her staring at me. I can smell her. She smells like a tart. Like the kind you would eat as a kid until your tongue bled raw.

"Are we comfortable?" the professor scolds. I nod with a wicked smile. Very.

As he continues his boring ass lecture about shit I already know, I glance in the direction of the girl.

She's prettier up close with her hair not hiding her face. She has freckles on her cheeks, and her skin appears to be so soft. She has brown eyes, the color you get when you mix chocolate and milk.

"I'm Sebastian." I wink at her. Her hot chocolate eyes drag to mine, and her cheeks blush. She has a Jennifer Aniston look about her. Down to earth.

"I'm Odette," she replies in a soft voice. Her mate clears his throat, and she stiffens.

He's really starting to piss me off. I feel like not only my respect, but my manhood is being challenged.

Challenge accepted, motherfucker.

"Oh my God!" Odette moans, her face pressed against the bathroom stall so hard, her cheek has to be nearly raw. Her skirt is pushed up over her smooth ass, her pink thong pulled to the side as I drive in and out of her heat. I have one of her legs hiked up while she tries to keep her balance on the other, allowing me to hit just a tad deeper.

"Yes! Just like that!" She grits through clinched teeth. Quickly, I wrap my hand around her mouth to quiet her and continue to hit it from the back. The stall rattles with each thrust, and the breath is knocked from her lungs. Her rosary beads flick against her neck as she commits the most common sin of all. My cock slides in and out of her wetness, and my balls squeeze, wanting to fill her with cum. I want her to return to her little boy toy full of my cum and smelling like me.

"Look at me," I demand. She turns her head as much as she can, those brown eyes finding mine. She blinks, and it angers me.

"Don't blink. I want you to always remember my face when you fuck someone. To only think of me and feel me inside you."

Her forehead wrinkles with unease.

"What?" she pants in confusion.

Taking one of my hands off her hip, I lick the tip of my finger, slide it down the crack of her ass, and press it into the little rose bud between her cheeks. Girls who have had more cock than they've had hot dinners never let a guy near their asshole, which means it will be more sensitive than her over abused g-spot.

Just as my finger makes contact, her knees go weak, and I drive the tip of my cock as deep as it can go.

Her pussy grips my cock like a vice, and her asshole tightens around my finger. She tries to lower her head, and I press my forehead against the side of her temple to steady her, to make her look me in the eye as she unravels like a spool of silk.

She will see my face when she fucks anyone else. My eyes, the heat of my breath on her neck, and my finger in her ass. Only me.

I cum, not hard, but enough to take the edge off. The slight pressure of warmth and pleasure spiking up my dick like a sparkler left out in the rain on the Fourth of July. It's slow, and not very impressive, but still something. I slowly pull out of her, leaving her to rest against the cool bathroom stall as I tie the end of the condom and flush it.

Shoving my dick back in my pants, I feel somewhat satisfied. She listened. She looked me in the eyes. And I got what I wanted: her to want me and not her boyfriend. But it was too easy. She let me fuck her like it was nothing, and that only goes to show how much value she has for herself—her self-worth. I need more in a woman. I want to feel like I can't breathe without that special someone.

"Wow," she murmurs.

I don't respond. Pulling my arm up, I glance at my watch. Shit, I have to meet that counselor bitch in ten minutes. Class is over, and I didn't even get to get in with the boys from The Elite.

"I've gotta go," I say, my tone dry.

She grabs my arm, stopping me.

"Wait, don't you want my number?" She wipes her hair from her flushed face.

"Nah, I don't think so, babe."

"Well, you'll be at the party tonight, right?" Desperation leaks into her voice, filling me with joy. This is all it took to take the place of the man she was just eye-fucking an hour ago. The ingrained refusal to follow up on any social events with a fuck has me nearly saying no, but I do want to find out more about The Elite.

"Will Rhett Masters or Samuel Gunner be there?" I contemplate.

She gives an uncertain look. "Probably Rhett. He's really good friends with the guy throwing it."

This would give me an inside look on how the chosen Elite live and act. I wasn't chosen, so I obviously don't live like them. If I'm going to blend in, I have to become my brothers.

"I might be there." I wink, then leave her in the bathroom.

Even if I do show up, I don't plan on fucking her again.

Back in Mrs. Griffin's office, or Lillian, as she wants me to call her, I wait for her to finish typing on her computer. My eyes slide down her silky neck to her breasts. I wonder if she's wearing the black bra from yesterday. Does she know I was watching her last night? Maybe she liked it. I bet that's why she took her bra off right in front of her window, on display for the whole neighborhood to see. She knew I was there.

My eyes fall on the donut and coffee on the corner of her desk, and she notices.

"Sweet tooth? Me too." Her tone drops low at the end, making me shift to relieve my semi hard cock.

Sighing, I sit up in my seat.

"I'd rather have some Adderall," I reply honestly. *Or some of you.* My mind is all over the fucking place, not where it needs to be: on The Elite.

"Ignoring me?" She laces her fingers together.

Twisting my watch on my wrist, I sigh, ready for this to be over with. "How is everything? How are you coping?"

"Coping?" My brows furrow in. She's starting to annoy me.

"With your roommate? Might be good to make new friends after losing the two in the fire."

Scoffing, I glance out the window, rubbing my chin.

"They weren't friends," I correct. I don't have any close friends, and what sort of counselor says shit like that?

"Still, it had to be hard to see someone die."

"Must it?" I taunt.

There's no crack in her tone or appearance. She's not uncomfortable. I like it when women squirm. I'm fucked up like that. Watching someone grow nervous by something I've said or done puts me in control.

Standing, her eyes widen as I take over the room.

"Seeing a stranger's flesh burning alive, hearing a female scream for help while you slowly drown?" I clarify. Is that what she thinks was so hard to see?

Rounding the desk, I toss my arm over her shoulder like we're best friends having pillow talk. She stiffens, goosebumps raising along the nape of her neck, but she doesn't falter under my intrusion of personal space.

Leaning closer, my lips brush against the fuzz of her ear.

"The only thing I can't cope with is how much of a waste it was to watch such a beautiful woman with poise and potential go without ever knowing what being truly loved was. "By me," I whisper in a tone so deep and low, it scrapes the bottom of my vocal cords.

Her head snaps in my direction, a crazy look flashing in her eyes. You know the look, the one where she wants to tell me I've lost it, that I'm not right in the head. I hear it all the time, and I like it. I'm finding it hard not to laugh in her face right now.

She smirks. Standing up, she walks to the window, her nails tapping on the sill, as if I don't affect her. What the fuck? Did I read her wrong?

"I admire ambition and drive. Sacrifices have to be made in life and accidents happen. We can't let the bad hold us back when it can propel us forward."

My brows furrow. Is she hinting at something?

"That will be all for today, but I'll be seeing you soon." Her voice is controlled.

"Yeah. I think so too." Winking at her, I stand up

straight, pressing my hands into the pockets of my slacks. I won't let her know she's getting in my head.

"Have a nice day, *Lillian*," I call out before whistling a tune close to the movie *Kill Bill*.

"You too…Envy."

"What?" I snap, my heart thundering in my chest.

"I said, you too, Henry."

My eyes narrow on her. "My name's Sebastian," I growl, and she fucking smirks, her head tilting to the side, studying me. "Oh, yes, sorry. It's crazy how easily names can become mixed up when I have so many to select from." She walks to where I'm standing and leans in so close, I can taste her breath when she says, "I'm usually very vigilant with my names. I'll remember yours from here on out."

Does she know I put my name on the list? *Fuck*.

VII

UINCENDUM NATUS

SIX

Heading back to my dorm, the smell of greenery slowly changes to the scent of popcorn. The bustle of student slows and lights begin to turn on as the sun starts its descend, warning the creatures of the south to take refuge. Sometimes, I wish I was a wild animal. The cycle of life is killing and surviving, being free to the point of living. Being a person...you're just told you're your own person, but really, the rules of society keep us caged. Living in a dorm is really starting to take its toll on me mentally. I give it a week before I start saying "bro."

Girls watch me from the corners of their eyes. They're scared of me, but turned on at the same time. That nibble of their bottom lip and nervous fidgeting of their fingers is almost enough to make me worry I come on too strong with my presence. Why, if it weren't for the long swish of

45

their tongue across their lips and the fuck me eyes, I'd almost think about redirecting my hard stares. Then again, maybe it's the way I hold my shoulders, confident and sure, that makes them insecure. Possibly because I'm not afraid to look someone in the eye in passing?

My lips twitch, but don't fully lift into a smile as I pass them all without any fucks to give. Their giggles and low whispers are cute, but unattractive. Girls—not women.

I notice Samuel Gunner pacing outside near my dorm, smoking a cigarette. He always looks fucking angry. That, and his leather jacket, top off the bad boy look he has going on.

Hands in my pocket, I walk up to him and bump into him on purpose. He spins around, his eyes heated.

"What the fuck?" he growls.

He suits his sin: angry and moody.

"Why so glum?" I smile, trying to brighten his mood. His brows narrow in on me, smoke billowing from his nostrils.

"Not now," he clips. When I first met him, he didn't have a lot to say and was pretty fucking rude. I'm starting to gather that's just the kind of guy he is. Angry.

Pulling my hand from my pocket, I wrap it around him, putting my weight on him. I feel like he wasn't hugged enough growing up. Maybe that's his problem.

"You should join me at the party tonight," I offer, even though I don't even know where said party is. I'm sure it can't be hard to find. Few beers, some women, he'll open right up to me.

"Pass." He shrugs out from underneath me and starts stomping off into the distance. What a prick. He's going to be hard to get close to. I shake my head and resume the path back to my room.

Inside the dorm, I head up the stairs. Steam billows out of the girls shower room, calling to me like a siren on a dark night. The smell of soap and flowers makes me stop and look through the steam. Girls of every feather walk around naked, talking and laughing. Nipples of every color, shape, and size cause my dick to twitch. My nails dig into my palm, wanting to grasp every fucking pair. I want to walk in there, drop my pants, and watch the girls drop to their knees, ready to please me. I'd be their God, and in return, they'd obey and love me like a woman should.

Droplets of water skim down the firm ass cheeks of the ones facing away, and I can't stop looking. Tan lines and dimples have me instantly wanting to fuck—now.

"Hey, man!" Tearing my gaze from the girls, Olly stands down the hall, waving at me like a dweeb, his laptop under one arm. He rushes over to me and fixes his glasses.

"I'm about to go to talk to a room allocation officer and see if I can get switched back with you," he says, but I ignore him. Wrapping my arm around him, I turn his body to face the open showers.

"Shut the fuck up and look," I say as I point. "That is all you need to be thinking about, Olly boy, and for fuck's sake, don't be asking to room with me—unless you like living in a closet." His mouth drops and his eyes widen as if it's the first time he's seen the majesticness of a woman's body. His expression mimics a teenage boy coming across his first porno.

Gripping his shoulder, I shove him back and forth.

"Oliver! You can't tell me you're a virgin," I groan at

my newfound clinger, then step us away from the door before some noble passerby tries to get heated about our staring.

"I'm waiting…you know." He clears his throat, feeling uncomfortable.

"For what?"

"That's what God wants…isn't it?" He pushes his glasses up his nose. Naive eyes look at me for all the answers. I am not the one to look up to, though.

I stroll to my room, and he follows me inside without an invitation.

"Have you heard about a party going on tonight?" I ask, deciding to change the subject and use him for info while he's here.

"Yeah. It's supposed to be at some rich guy's place. They call him God or something." He snorts, as if it's the most ridiculous thing he's ever heard. God is Gluttony. Which means I need to be at this party for sure. I need to get on his good side.

"Don't you have the party app?" Oliver looks up at me like I'm an airhead.

"Party app?" What the fuck is that?

"They handed out flyers everywhere." He acts as if I've been living in a closet. I give him a look of confusion. I try to avoid the people handing shit out.

He huffs, holding his hand out expectantly.

"Let me see your phone." Pulling it out of my pocket, I hand it over to him, and he scrunches his nose before uploading something.

Glancing at the app, I find the address to God's house. Olly sits down on his old bed before opening his laptop. He's making himself too comfortable.

"You should come," I tell Oliver.

He looks up at me like a puppy who just found its new owner. "You wanna go together?"

"No, I have plans." I quirk a brow. He's becoming annoying. I can't have the real Envy lurking around me like a bad smell. I drop my ass into my computer chair, my arm nudging the mouse, making the monitor turn on.

Olly turns his attention to my computer. "The Elite? I've heard of them," he announces. My eyes snap to my computer, seeing my search up in big fucking letters. The Elite symbol there beneath it, fucking proud on my screen.

Shit, he wasn't supposed to see that. In fact, Olly is just too close to this stuff. If he knows about The Elite, it's only a matter of time before he realizes I'm a candidate. Does he know he was a candidate? What if he figures out he was on the list? I can't have that happen. Can't have this little shit ruining everything for me. My mind disappears into that dark place. Where right and wrong don't exist.

Oliver Olly needs to go.

"For a geek, you have a shitty computer." I change the subject, cracking my neck back and forth.

He glares at me.

"I put this together myself," he informs me pointedly.

"Ha. I can tell." Shaking my head, I step to my closet and look for something more casual to wear. Some light washed jeans, white sneakers, and a dark blue button-up. *Think...*

"What are you, some kind of know-it-all about computers or something?" Oliver fires back.

"Some say so," I murmur, buttoning up my shirt. *Think...*

"Oh yeah, what kind of laptop do you have?"

"I prefer my built desktop at home, but here I have my Alien." *Think...*

"You have something better than an Alien?" He does that scrunching thing with his nose again, followed by heavy breathing. I nod.

"You must know your way around a keyboard." He chuckles. That's the first time I've heard that. I've been told I know my way around a woman's body, but a keyboard...that's just fucking weird to hear.

"All right, Bill Gates, I'm out. Time for you to go." Glancing in the mirror, I run my fingers through my hair, slicking it back, my bottle green eyes dancing at what the evening holds. I have this excited feeling running through me, making me feel almost high. That's a good sign. Tonight's going to be awesome.

Oliver can be tomorrow's problem.

"You sure you don't want to go together?" he asks again, almost desperate. It's kinda sad. I bet he's not going to go unless he comes with me, but it's not my fucking problem.

I step out of my room and lock the door behind me. "I don't think we'll be running in the same circles," I state before walking away.

When I get to the end of the corridor, I look back to see Oliver striding his way down the opposite hall. The idea that he might think I'm in The Elite is not settling well with me. Waiting 'til tomorrow is too long. What if he tells someone or ruins this whole fucking thing for me?

I watch as he goes into his room. He leaves the door open, and is back out in the hall in seconds. A small shower bag and robe under one arm, his computer still attached to him and a power cord. *What the fuck are you doing?*

He moves toward the shower room, sticking his power cord in the outlet just outside and disappearing.

Awww, Olly, my boy...going back to the showers to stalk the girls I see. I'd almost be proud if I wasn't nervous as fuck you were a rat.

Standing outside the shower room, my back to the wall, I turn my good ear to hear what he's doing. The shower head begins to spray, and he begins whistling out of tune to a soft melody echoing through the room. The familiar sound of the curtain sliding across the metal rod has my feet in motion.

The steamy shower room is empty apart from Oliver's things set out on the counter and his form hidden behind a curtain. My eyes skim over his laptop playing music while he showers. Rubbing my chin, I look over my shoulder at the shower, then back to the computer. He has a long fucking cord attached to this thing, charging. I bet it would stretch across the room.

Sorry, Olly man.

Snatching a pair of his nail scissors from his shower kit, I expose the live wire on the charger and pick the laptop off the counter. I whip the curtains open, the metal bar falling into the stall with him. Olly screams in a high-pitched voice, his dick in his hand while he gets his rocks off, no doubt to the girls he was watching moments before.

"Catch," I throw the laptop at him. His wet fingers slip and slide along the top, and it falls in the ever-clogging drain of the shower. The live wire disappears beneath the slow draining water. It sparks and bursts. Olly tenses, his eyes wide. *It actually fucking worked.* Nobody will even question a geek with his laptop on in the shower, dick in hand. It's the perfect staged accident.

The lights in the room begin to flicker and zap, and I quickly make my way out of the shower room and back to the mission at hand. The party—The Elite.

VII

UINCENDUM NATUS

SEVEN

God, aka Baxter Goddard the Fifth, is loaded with money to the point of not caring. With a name like that, I didn't expect anything less. The party is on a plantation, with waitstaff and a live band. It reminds me of a house on the show *True Blood*. Creepy, but in a rich kind of way. The party is packed full of good people. The way they laugh, smile, and step to the beat of the music. Common. Basic. Nothing at all like me.

A waitress passes by, giving me a knowing smile as she looks me over. I snatch two red cups from her tray and give her a sly wink. Taking my first sip of the night, suds fill my mouth as my gaze takes in the more risqué scene starting to unfold as half-dressed girls dance, men sliding up behind them and running their hands over their curves.

Dancing is actually something I'm good at. Back in my

high school years, a former classmate wanted to be prom king, but so did I. So I took dance classes and showed my moves off before the time to vote. Every girl in the school wanted me to ask them to prom.

Taking another sip, I decide to look the place over before joining on the dancefloor. I'm on a mission, after all. Causally drinking my beer, I follow the sound of splashing to a big ass pool. Of course he has a pool. I'm sure he has tennis courts and a massage room too. Fucking rich pricks.

Before I know it, I've finished one of the solo cups and am on my second. My uncle would disapprove of my drinking. It brings out my crazy side, he says. I'm fine, though. It's just a couple drinks.

A hand caresses my arm, grabbing my attention. A girl with long blonde hair and vixen-green eyes smiles at me. She's new.

Her short denim shorts ride up just enough to see the swell of her ass, and that black top that hangs off both her shoulders is sexy. There's something about a bare, tan shoulder. She's cute.

Before she pulls away from my arm, I grasp her hand and tug her close. Where does she think she's going?

"Wanna dance?" I ask, having enough of looking the house over.

She smiles, her teeth white and lips the color of pink cotton candy.

She glances over her shoulder as if she's looking for permission from someone before finally nodding. Lacing my fingers with hers, I tuck her hand behind my back and lead her to the dance floor where everyone is getting personal and sweaty. They're secluded to their own island of dry humping, and it angers me that any of these woman would want to dance with these guys rather than myself. I'll show them.

Chugging the last of my drink, I toss the cup to the floor and pull her chest flush with mine, her arms wrapping around my neck. Her body begins to move, her hips swaying side to side. Sliding my hand down her arm, I bend at the knees and dance to the rhythm of her body.

"Tuesday" by Ilovemakonnen blares from the speakers, the bass making my chest vibrate.

Closing my eyes, I can't help but smell her. The scent of something sweet, like candy, fills my nostrils. Mmm. I could get used to that smell on my clothes. A tap on my shoulder has me straightening, my eyes wide. My candy girl's sweet expression turns sour. She shrugs, then pulls away from me, as if Daddy just caught her having a good time and she has to leave. My brows narrow in on her. Where the fuck does she think she's going? That's when a cold rush of air pulls through my nostrils. A man in a letterman jacket is tugging her away from me. Who is this cat? A boyfriend?

He wraps his arm around her and glares over his shoulder at me with a look conveying he will always be her number one. I grit my teeth. An unwanted mist of insecurity washes over me, and I don't like it.

I hate people like him. They think they're better—that they can take whatever they want from me.

Another waitress sashays by, and I grab two more cups, my eyes penetrating the fucker who just took my chick for the night. I'm pissed. I *should* stop drinking. I *should* leave.

Taking up a dark corner, I cross my arms and stew

over that prick. My mind starts to race on what I should have done to that football player. Sip after sip, I become more and more angry. I should do something about that motherfucker. He made me look like a chump. The thought of releasing my rage on his face is very tempting. I'd wrap both my hands around his esophagus and snap every fucking bone, but then I'd lose my chance of cementing my place in The Elite and end up getting arrested—again.

"Hey!" A beam of a smiling girl is placed directly in my line of sight.

Honey hair, chocolate eyes. Odette. She's wearing a black dress with black chucks.

Taking a drink from my cup, my eyes meet hers over the rim. I was hoping I wouldn't run into her again.

"I dumped my boyfriend," she says, a little too eagerly. This is exactly why I didn't want to see her.

"I didn't ask you to do that," I clip out.

She shrugs.

"It was time."

"Look, nothing will come from you standing here chatting me up. You're just not my type." Her face pales, my boldness too much for her to handle.

Wrapping my arm around her neck, I pull her close. Her skin doesn't feel as soft as it had earlier. A light bulb goes off inside my head.

"But I can never have enough friends." I grin at her, the beer starting to hit my system. She lights up, and it occurs to me this poor girl may not have any friends. Just fuck buddies.

"So, you wanna help a friend get revenge?" I nudge her a little closer, getting friendly. She holds onto my wrist wrapped around her waist and nibbles on her bottom lip.

"Who?"

Solo cup still in my hand, I point across the way toward dick-face in the letterman jacket.

"Chip?" Her voice raises in excitement. He has a name. Chip. How fucking stupid. "He's into some weird shit. I hate that guy!" she sneers, as if she just ate something bad.

"Yeah?"

"One time—"

She begins to go into detail about how he broke her heart, yada, yada. From the sound of it, Odette lets anyone in her pants, then gets upset when they don't love her and walk away. I can relate.

"Great!" My voice rises a little too loudly. I can't help but feel annoyed at her chipper attitude. I never thought she was going to shut up. "Here's what I want you to do. Go make a move on him, and be...bold about it." A smile crosses my face, one that scares even me as I think about what I'm about to do to that shit-stain. I need Odette to listen if this is going to work. Nobody makes a fool of Sebastian Westbrook—especially some fucking cliché jock.

"Like...you want me to sleep with him or something?" She chews on her pinky nail, watching Chip from afar. I'd say yes, but I don't want to spook her.

"Whatever works. Just get him upstairs."

"And what's in it for me? Maybe you can take me out sometime?"

Smiling my cocksure grin, I shrug, "Sure."

She nods, then heads his way like a good little soldier. I hide my excitement behind another sip of beer. This is going to be perfect. I'm already starting to feel better about the evening.

Odette knows how to get a guy. A soft touch on the elbow. Her eyes fluttering with delight as she laughs like he just said something funny even though we both know nothing the guy has to say is humorous. Her tongue sliding across her bottom lip, giving it that wet, sexy look that would hook any man.

Chip laughs, caught in her web of seduction. Good.

She leans in, whispering to him, and he glances around before crumpling his cup and heading upstairs, Odette in tow.

"Playtime," I murmur, tossing the rest of my drink to the floor. Taking my time up the stairs, I pull out my phone, unlock it, and get it ready for my plan of attack. A flash of honey hair disappears behind a door to the far left, and I stride up to it, standing just outside, whistling in waiting.

"Three. Two. One…" I crack the door open to see if Odette is working her magic. At the sound of panting, I push my phone through the small opening, click record, and Bluetooth it to the house's TV system. Odette is on her knees, her head sliding back and forth, his dick deep in her mouth. Her hair swishes across her back, and he grips it at the base as he pumps his hips into her face.

"God, you suck dick like no other, Odette," he groans, the sound of his voice echoing throughout the house.

I chuckle, continuing to record. Fuck, this is too easy.

"Spank my ass. Spank it, you naughty little bitch!" Chip grunts before a loud smack sounds through the house.

Laughter downstairs lifts through the air, and I know

my job is done. Snatching my phone from the door, I slam it, letting Odette know I have what I need. *Good girl.*

God, I feel like the fucking devil right now, but that's how winning works.

Seconds pass before Odette steps out of the room, wiping her mouth off and smiling at me. Just in time for candy girl to stomp upstairs, a flushed expression on her face, looking for her cheating boyfriend.

"Chip!" she screams, pounding on each door, demanding entry. I could easily have her if I wanted. It would serve that fucker right. But I need to get back to the mission at hand. Playtime is over.

"Who fucked with the TVs?" a male voice barks as I hit the last step of the stairs. A big man. Confident eyes meet mine, and I instantly know it's God. I lift my chin at him.

"Did you do this?" he asks, rubbing the stubble on his chin.

I shrug, unable to help the evil grin spreading across my face. He gives me a look of credit, his lips smirked to the side and eyes prideful. I slide up next to him, throwing my arm around his neck. He tenses, but doesn't shove me away.

"If anyone, then, knows the good they ought to do and doesn't do it, it is sin for them," I say, reciting James 4:17.

I know some words of the big man upstairs, I just don't abide by them often.

His eyes shoot to mine again, and it's then I know I have his attention. I've impressed him.

"Name's Sebastian."

"No! I don't want to hear it, Chip! I knew you were

a piece of shit!" Candy Lips screams from upstairs. Shit's really starting to hit the fan. *Should have stayed on the dance-floor with me, sweet cheeks.*

"Time for me to go, God." Twisting the watch on my wrist, I make my exit, feeling like a fucking God myself.

VII

UINCENDUM NATUS

EIGHT

Waking up, I almost forget where I am, but the small, stiff bed beneath me serves as an instant reminder. Rubbing my forehead with both hands, I yawn, still tired. Maybe I shouldn't have hit that party up last night. I don't even remember how I got home. Hopefully I didn't steal a car or kill anyone. I did get on God's good side, though. It's encouraging to know that maybe I do belong in The Elite. Sitting up, I toss my legs over the bed. I could use some coffee...or cocaine. Maybe both.

I scratch at my bare chest, eyeing the window, the sun shining through way too fucking early. My old place had black-out curtains. The sheer fabric of these are more for decoration than anything. I'm really starting to miss my place.

Standing up, I grab some sweats from the closet and tug them on. Slipping on my house shoes, I step into the hall on the hunt for some coffee. It's too fucking lively for eight in the morning. People whispering, talking, and cuddling each other.

"What's going on?" I frown. I'm not a morning person, and it's taking everything I have not to turn around and go back to bed.

"A boy died in the shower room last night," a girl tells me, pulling her robe tight around herself.

Oh, shit. Olly. I forgot about him.

"What happened to him?" I feign shock, placing a hand to my chest and shaking my head.

"He was listening to his laptop or something. Accidental electrocution." She winces.

Perfect. Everyone thinks is was a horrific accident.

Downstairs, I find the main room Olly talked about the other day. Some old leather loveseats that look like they belong in a modern coffee house sit close to each other, a plush rainbow rug in between them, offset by old school wooden end tables.

Just beyond the hippie circle sits a green stove top, sink, and refrigerator. I think it looks second hand, but to the eyes of an interior designer, they'd say it was a twist on modern day art and the sixties. Shit, I bet they paid a ton just for that couch to look vintage.

My eyes fall on the coffee pot next to the sink full of dishes. Empty.

"Fuck!" I bark out loud, gaining everyone's attention.

I narrow my eyes at them all, then head back up the stairs to fetch a shirt or something. I'll just go to a fucking Starbucks.

ENVY

Yawning, I pull on a blue polo, and reach for my watch sitting in its box. My eyes shift to the coffee cup next to it. I raise my brow in confusion, wondering if I brought it in last night. I wrap my hand around it.

"Warm."

I lift the cup to smell the brew, finding a shiny gold coin resting beneath it. A skull with a crown engraved into it. The Elite's emblem. Taking the coin in hand, I flip it over. "The Elite Seven" is etched into the back.

"What the fuck?" I mutter, at a loss for words. I'd remember if someone gave this to me last night. Excitement buzzes through my body. This better not be a joke. I look around my room for the person responsible for placing the coin, but I'm alone.

This is too damn easy. With this coin comes the opportunity for power, respect, money, and I bet I'll find a worthy woman now—one to carry my name, to accept a rose just from me—to clutch it in her teeth while I pound into her, claiming her as my own.

I did this, I made this happen for me. If I make it to the end, I'll have everything I've ever wanted in life.

A folded-up piece of paper placed under my phone gains my attention. Pushing my phone to the side, I pick it up and open it. It's coordinates of some kind. I flip the paper over for more info, but there's nothing. It's to the point, and very secretive. This has to be real. Placing my name on the list of the chosen Elite worked. The urban fucking legend has risen from the tombs and chose me as one of their members.

VII

UINCENDUM NATUS

NINE

One Week Later

The coordinates brought me to an old nunnery where I officially met the others. We vowed to a brotherhood and agreed to complete a task to earn our place officially. I faintly remember drinking from a cup to embrace our newfound family, but I can't remember much after that. All I know is I'm in the fucking Elite. I have a brotherhood. A goal in life. A family.

But now, a week later, shit got real quick. I'm sitting in a cramped car with my fellow brothers after almost dumping a body—Rhett's dad. They got in a fight and Rhett needed his brothers for a solution. We were supposed to be getting rid of his dead body, but the fucker wasn't dead and these sinful bastards apparently have morals after all. Letting him live was a boring way to end a night if you ask me. I would have fed him to the alligators just for fun.

"You should have just let me kill him. You wouldn't have to worry about him anymore," I tell Rhett as we all bounce around in the vehicle. I had my knife ready, seconds away from ending the motherfucker. God gives me a quizzical look, but doesn't speak.

"What is wrong with you?" Sam asks from beside me, and I laugh, throwing my arm around him.

"Oh, Sammy," I state in a mocking tone. He shoves me off him, his angry demeanor not lacking any.

"Only my sister calls me Sammy." He glares at me, and I pause, letting the memory of his sister wash over me.

"We should do something tonight. Let's go out," I say to the brothers. I feel high right now, excited.

"I'm down." Rhett shrugs, drinking his soda. "I need a high, and bonding with our brothers is what we're supposed to be doing, right?"

"Right," I shout, clapping him on the shoulder. My heart begins to pound manic in my chest when my eye catches a female coming toward us.

Long brown hair laying like silk across her shoulders, gray eyes finding me, thick, plump lips lifting into a smile. It's like the world has slowed and it's just me and her. She stops at our table and hands something to Wrath. "You forgot your wallet this morning." She turns, but not before her eyes track Rhett, then move to me.

"Who was that?" I ask, getting to my feet, my eyes never leaving the sway of her body as she sashays away.

"My sister, so stop checking out her ass," Sam growls.

"She gave me that look," I say in awe.

"If it was the look of staring at a dead man, you're right,"

Wrath warns, throwing his food at me.

"Does she go here?" I ask, needing to know everything about her.

Jumping to his feet, Wrath grabs me in a playful headlock. I jab his ribs, and we mess around until Sam releasse me and fucks off.

Picking up my bag, I ask Rhett, "Where should we meet?"

"My house. I'll text the address."

"I already know where it is," I inform him, then still. *Shit, is it weird I know that? Is he frowning at me?*

"Stalk much?" he snorts, throwing his trash away. *I don't know what to say to that.*

"I'm kidding. Meet me around nine." *He relieves me of the awkward tension. I wave him off and race inside to see if I can find the angel.*

It doesn't take me long. It's like fate wants us to be together.

I catch her in the corridor getting a soda from the machine. Her soft, round face smiles in the most delicate way as she waves at some guy. My chest constricts at the attention she's giving him. Her hair falls down her back angelically, and I itch to feel it wrapped around my hand in the throes of ecstasy. That goddamn pink and white dress that falls just to her knees, showing her creamy skin, is tortuous to mankind. And to make it worse—she doesn't even know it.

I want—no, I need—to know her name. It's as if she walked right out of a romantic comedy, so sweet and innocent looking, but she holds the bounty of sin in those eyes.

Her gaze slowly casts forward before resting on mine, and my mouth suddenly feels dry. The thoughts of what I've always wanted drum in my head.

I could love this woman. She could love me. Yeah, she could be the one.

ENVY

Her lips part as she smiles in the friendliest way.

Walking up behind her, I can't help but introduce myself.

"Hey! I didn't catch your name!" I say, coming to rest next to her. She turns, an angelic smile on her face.

"Are you lost?" She tucks a stray hair behind her ear, her tart tone trying to tack on an attitude.

"Uh…" I anxiously rub the back of my neck, my watch sliding down my wrist in the act. "I guess you could say that." Is this a trick? Is God really putting this beautiful creature in my hands?

"You're one of my brother's friends, aren't you?" She chuckles. Fuck me, she's too cute. I'm going to do things to this girl she'll never forget. She walked right into my web.

"Not if it means I can't talk to you." She's beautiful. Her skin reminds me of lotion and honey, so creamy and soft looking. I want to hurt her and love her at the same time. The conflicting feeling makes me feel chaotic.

"I'm Sabella." She blushes, and I instantly get a flutter in my dick. She's interested.

"I'm Sebastian. Maybe you can help me find my way around this town sometime." I offer her my innocent eyes.

And that's all it takes to get her number.

VII

UINCENDUM NATUS

TEN

Looking at the flowers on display at the store, my eyes feast on the red roses, my mind flitting back to my uncle and his mistress.

My hand hovers above them, wanting to get one for Sabella, but my chest constricts. No, it's not time for those. Yet.

I settle for the simple daisies. She looks like a daisy kind of girl. Delicate, sweet, and summery.

Pulling my phone out, I check to make sure she hasn't canceled our coffee date. No texts so far, so all is good. Hopefully Sam stays busy with his task so he doesn't interrupt mine and Sab's time together. I mean, I gave him more than enough shit to keep him busy—Patience's address, email passwords, whereabouts. He should have it handled.

ENVY

Pulling my sleeves up to my elbows, the heat from the Louisiana sun causing me to sweat, I walk faster to the coffee shop. I'm glad she chose a place close by to meet up. It would be embarrassing as fuck to tell her I don't have a car. Maybe The Elite will hook me up with one. I mean, I can't do tasks without one.

Finally reaching the small coffee shop, Topped Off, I head inside, the bell jingling as I enter. It smells of strong coffee beans and muffins.

There are small coffee tables and booths surrounding the walls, and in the center of the room sits a blue and green couch with a rectangle coffee table in the middle.

Sabella sits on the blue couch, her legs crossed beneath her yellow sundress. Her hair frames her innocent face before cascading down her shoulders just in front of her breasts.

Clearing my throat, I head her way.

She's aware of my presence and looks up, her gray eyes smiling.

"Sebastian." She stands and hugs me. God, she smells so good, like fresh laundry.

"Uh, these are for you." I hand her the flowers.

"Oh my, you shouldn't have!" She blushes and takes them before sitting down. I sit across from her on the green couch.

"You know, I almost didn't agree to this," she replies meekly, setting the flowers beside her.

"Hmm. How come?" I give in, fishing.

"With you being my brother's friend and all," she says, matter of fact.

"I guess I can't be his friend then." I laugh, amused she thinks I'd already be up for dating.

"It's just...Sammy is very protective, and he might not like us being friends," she tries to explain. I can see that about Sam. He's already threatened me to stay away from Sabella more times than I can count—none of which have worked. And I plan on being more than "friends."

"We don't have to tell him anything." I shake my head, rubbing my chin with my index finger. "This is just coffee anyway, right?" I clarify.

She nods a little to eagerly. "Exactly!"

She's so damn cute and small. I wonder if she's a virgin. It makes my dick twitch.

"So, tell me about yourself. What do you do for fun?" she asks, re-crossing her legs.

Stalk people like you.

"Uh, I like to fiddle with computers I guess you could say." I sit up, resting my elbows on my knees.

"Oh, I'm such a klutz when it comes to those things." She giggles, and I feel that little laugh all the way to my dick.

Just then, a barista takes the opportunity to step in.

"Can I get you two anything?" he asks. My eyes slide up his ugly green apron to his buggy blue eyes. I'm annoyed he's interrupted us, but he's just doing his job.

"Just a cup of coffee," I order.

"Iced coffee for me, please." She smiles at him, her manners coming through.

I don't know about this girl. She might be too sweet for me. I'd easily break her.

"My father says coffee is going to give me diabetes someday." She makes small talk.

"You and your dad close?" She lowers her head, and I instantly know I've hit a sore subject.

"Not really. Things are complicated in my house." Her face scrunches, her eyes avoiding mine. With Sam being her brother, I could see things being really difficult. The guy is fucking angry about everything.

The barista sets our coffees down on the table and ducks out of the way. Good. Less chat from him means less of a distraction.

Sabella uncrosses her legs and re-crosses them again before picking up her coffee like a princess would a cup of tea.

"What about you, are you and your parents close?"

Blowing the heat from the top of my coffee, I give a tight smile.

"Sure," I lie. Who wants to hear a man talk about his dead parents?

"That's great to hear." She takes a sip of her coffee, her lips forming around the straw in ways that has my dick twitching.

Silence falls between us. I tug my phone out and toss a text her way to break the ice.

Me: Just be yourself. It's just me.

Her phone dings, and she picks it up off the couch cushion. Her eyes meet mine when she realizes it's from me.

She smiles, and sets the phone down.

"Tell me about your brother," I suggest, knowing it's easier for her to open up about him than anyone else.

"He's really incredible once you get to know him. Very loyal, but nobody wants to look past his flaws to see the good in him." She swirls the coffee in her cup, her voice cracking with agitation.

"I can see that," I sympathize.

"You know, I think he might be seeing someone. He's been so secretive lately. I just wish I knew who it was." Her eyes focus forward as she becomes lost in her own thoughts.

Sam with a girlfriend? That's a scary thought. It's like the Hulk trying to pet a fucking bird.

Her phone chimes, and she gives me a look.

"Not me this time." I chuckle, making her smile again, but my body is tense as fuck wondering who the hell is texting her. Looking at the screen of her cell, her cute expression dulls, her cheery face taking a turn.

"I have to go."

I stand. "Oh?"

So soon? I'm not done with her.

"Looks like Sam is up to no good again," she grumbles, snatching her things from the couch in haste. Fucking Sam.

"Everything okay?"

"I'm sure it will be." She stops, standing in front of me like she wants to hug me, but thinks better of it.

"Thanks so much for meeting up. We should do this again." She nods as she looks up at me.

"For sure. I'd like that." Reaching forward, I tuck a strand of her hair behind her ear and notice her nipples pebble beneath her dress.

"I can make you dinner?" she offers.

"I'd never turn down a homecooked meal." I grin.

She hugs me, and I inhale her scent one last time.

Until we meet again, supple flower.

She walks away, and my hand rolls into a fist. Fucking Sam getting in the middle of things is a distraction I'm not okay with. I don't like him taking up Sabella's attention.

ENVY

Sabella was right about one thing, though. He is seeing someone. Sam has asked me several times to help him figure out the girl that has become his task. Using my hacking skills to find out where she lives, and who she is. Who knows, maybe if I play my cards right, Sabella and I will be on double dates with brother dearest.

Something in my chest swells at the thought, and a smile rises to my face. Wouldn't that be fucking awesome. Sam—my Elite brother and maybe my brother-in-law. We'd double date and have barbeques on the weekend, watch football together and shoot the shit. I swallow down my excitement. It's too soon to be thinking about all that, but Sabella said she wanted to do this again. She hugged me—that has to mean something.

Everything is really starting to work out perfectly.

VII

UINCENDUM NATUS

ELEVEN

The next day

Sitting next to Sam in class, my attention bounces back and forth between him and Professor Pulliver. Sam has been going on about his new toy, Patience. Fuck, it's like she's his girlfriend rather than his task. It seems like ever since we all got into The Elite, the boys have all gotten girlfriends—everyone accept me.

"I don't know, things are different with her," Sam continues. "I really like her, you know?"

"You're starting to sound like Rhett," I grumble. My brothers are pussy whipped.

"Hey, did you hear anything about his task?" Sam changes the subject. Thank fuck.

"Nah, why?" I shrug, twisting my watch on my wrist.

"Heard he was having a hard time completing it is all."

I shake my head. I think Sam is having a hard time with his task too. He's mentioned a few times that he's really into Patience. From what I've read online, she's the daughter of the mayor. I can understand him not wanting to hurt her. Makes me wonder what else I can do for him. He's my brother, a friend, and I can't let him fail. Maybe another night of pizza at his place and some booze will help loosen him up.

Sam goes back to the subject of Patience and how they fuck nonstop. My nails dig into my palm as I think about how fucking horny I am. I'd do anything to bend his sister over right now.

Glancing across the room, my eyes fall on Micah, Greed. He's sitting alone near the front, tapping his pencil against his lips. He sure is different than the rest of us, rough around the edges. He's one I haven't gotten much time to hang out with.

Grabbing my shit, I decide to get to know him and bail on Sam and his third fuck story.

"Hey, I'll catch you later," I tell him before striding up a few rows and plopping down next to Micah. His cold eyes move to mine, and I smile.

"Hey, brother." He doesn't say anything, just situates himself in his chair. He seems almost feral, like a stray cat backed into a corner. He looks bored as fuck too. This clearly isn't his scene. "You wanna get out of here, go get a beer or something?"

This grabs his attention. Without a word, he's packing up his shit and standing, and I do the same.

Stepping out of the class, the wind blows a hot breeze, making me roll my sleeves up to my elbows. Micah runs his hand over his head, glaring out amongst those walking around us. His hair is short, close shaven to the scalp and around the sides, but a little longer on top. With his hard expression and tattoos, he looks like he just escaped prison. I would normally push my friendly self on him, wrap my arm around his shoulders and insist he open up to me, but I'm a little afraid of this guy. He might be more fucked up in the head than I am based on what I've seen on his social media.

"You don't talk much, do you?" With a quick glance over his shoulder, he tells me all I need to know. I shut the fuck up and continue walking beside him.

Everyone seems to step out of his way. They're afraid of him, and I understand why. He gives off a vibe that if I didn't know he came from wealth would make me wonder how the fuck he got into this college in the first place. Maybe he would have cheated his way in like me.

He walks us away from the campus, me doing most of the talking until we reach some dive bar. It's a brick building with one window and one door. The smell of beer and fried food wafts around the place. If I'm going to get mugged today, I'd want Micah by my side, I suppose.

Tugging the door open, we stride inside and find a seat at the bar. The lighting is dim at best. You can't even see in the far back corner.

Micah moves around the place as smooth as the smoke. He holds up two fingers to the bartender, and the older man wearing a stained apron barely reaching around his robust torso slides two brews down the bar to us.

"You come here often?" I ask, and Micah sighs before nodding. Taking a sip of my beer, I glance at the muted color of liquor stacked along the back wall behind the bar.

ENVY

I decide to confide in him a bit, see if that makes him open up some.

"I don't usually like myself when I drink. I become an arrogant asshole." I raise my voice in attempt to speak over the laughter in the back and jukebox.

Micah chuckles.

"I think we're all assholes. It's the one thing all of us Elite might have in common." He finally talks. I laugh, taking a drink with him. My nail picks at the crater in the marble top of the counter, my mind searching for something to break the ice.

"Did you hear Rhett is having trouble with his task?"

Micah's brows furrow as he takes another gulp.

"Yeah, I don't think he wants to do it from what Sam was going on about." I shrug.

"Have you gotten your task yet?" Micah questions.

I shake my head.

"I'm ready for whatever it is, though."

"Me too," he agrees. A hot little number near the end of the bar has her eye on either me or Micah. It's probably me. She has red hair that curls down and around her collarbone, a small tank top dipping into her bust, and a diamond necklace that shines in the shadiest part of the bar. Her body language seems confidant, but her eyes are troubled. Heavy laughter over my shoulder has me glancing back as someone knocks into Micah, causing him to spill his beer across the bar top.

"Hey, man!" Micah jumps up from his stool, pissed.

The man who knocked into him squares his shoulders, eyeing Micah. The dude is obviously a local if the alligator belt and boots are any indication.

"What the fuck is your problem, man?" Crocodile

Dundee slurs past his snaggle tooth.

Micah smirks, finding this guy amusing. Flicking his nose, he shoves the dude out of his personal space.

"You're my fucking problem!" Micah grunts. The man nearly flies on his ass with ease, no match for Micah.

"You want some more, you fucking pussy?" Micah starts after him, and I grab him by the shoulders in an attempt to stop him from killing the asshole.

"Easy, brother. Let's go somewhere else," I say, trying to calm the beast. He shoves me off, spewing hate at the local. The bartender demands we leave, but the entire place is in an uproar.

Managing to get myself between Micah and Snaggle Tooth, I start pushing Micah toward the door.

"He's not worth it, man." I pat him on the back, almost to the door.

"Yeah, you and your butt-buddy better leave before you really piss me off."

I stop, anger constricting my chest at the homophobic slur.

Turning on my heel, I squint and glare at the fucking redneck.

"What did you just call me?" My jaw clenches, my fingers caressing my chin.

"You heard me," he hiccups, trying to point at me and Micah.

I look over my shoulder at Micah and chuckle, feeling flushed.

"This guy?" I jut my thumb toward the drunk fuck, Micah looking at me, confused. Like a match snapping into its eternal flame, I turn and throw a fist into the man's mouth. Micah is by my side in seconds, fighting off one of the man's buddies. Stools are knocked over, the sound of skin and bone echoing over the chaos.

"GET OUT OF MY BAR!" sounds from above, and I freeze with my arm wrapped around a man's head. Micah punches someone in the face once more just for good measure before looking up.

The bartender is standing on the bar with a spatula and pot, glaring at us all.

"Now, I called the cops. You all best be leaving," he informs everyone.

I drop the sack of shit to the floor, and Micah grabs his stuff off the bar, both of us making quick work of getting out of here. I don't know who the owner called the cops on, but I'm not sticking around to find out.

Just outside, we hustle our way up a few blocks to get away from the area, my heart pounding in my chest. My knuckle is bleeding from hitting that snaggle tooth motherfucker in the mouth. That shit was intense—way better than sticking around for a fucking lecture.

Micah rubs his hand over his head and smiles at me.

"You ain't too bad, Envy."

I nod. "When you get your task, let me know if you need anything, brother." I lift my chin, letting him know I'm not just anybody. I'm in this with him. Besides, if all the brothers back down from their tasks, what does that mean for The Elite?

My phone chimes, and I dig it out, still out of breath.

Sab: Hey, you want to meet up?

"Hey, man, thanks for the fun. I better get going," Micah tells me before I even have a chance to reply to Sab. I do want to see her, but I also enjoy hanging with my brothers. The bond we have is forever growing, and it makes me feel undefeated with them by my side. However, after kicking some ass, I'm down for some pussy. God, just thinking about that naive little cunt of hers has an overwhelming pull and desire in me to want to destroy her innocence. I've checked her Facebook ten times today, but she hasn't posted once. I feel neglected not knowing what she's doing. I want to know everything about her, and if she's thinking of me. One fucking post saying she's met a great guy named Sebastian or something would be ideal.

"Yeah, see you around, man." I lift my chin and head back toward the school, replying to Sab. Pussy for the win.

VII

UINCENDUM NATUS

TWELVE

Back at campus, I find the beautiful Sabella on a bench under a tree. The wind blows a light breeze, causing billowing trees to dance shadows amongst her. She's wearing a cotton blue dress with white flats today, her nose stuck in a book. She looks like Belle from *Beauty and the Beast*. How fitting. The beauty and the beast. Only... my endings never fall on happy notes.

Rubbing my chin, I head her way, and like always, she senses me before seeing me. Her delicate eyes gaze above the spine of her book.

"Sebastian!" she greets happily, standing to hug me. I wrap my arms around her and smell her. Fresh laundry. My dick has grown to love that scent. I can't stand in the laundry room without getting a hard-on.

"Hey, is everything okay?" I ask in my most gentle

tone, when really, all I want to do is tangle my hand in her hair and kiss her stupid.

"Yeah, just a rough day. Wanted to see a friendly face, I guess." She waves me off, tucking her dress under her before sitting back on the bench.

"We could have met in your bed if you really wanted to get friendly." I wink, and her face pales. She clears her throat and begins to fiddle with her book nervously. Shit, she didn't like that. She's not like other girls I talk to. They usually like the arrogant dirty talk.

But that only makes me want her more.

I fucking knew she was special. Different from all the other girls.

"I was just playing, Sab." I run my finger over her arm, reassuring her my intentions are noble. Her head snaps up, gray eyes finding mine.

"Oh." She chuckles. There she is. Looks like I'm going to have to work for this one. I like that about her. She's already standing above the rest of the women in my life.

"So, what's going on?"

Her face takes a dip of innocence, and it kills me from the inside out. I want to hold her, get close. In any other situation, I'd slide up next to her, grab her by the hip, and kiss her worries away. But I can't. Instead, I rest my hand on top of hers, letting her know I'm here for her.

"Is it Wra—Sam?" Shit, I need to make sure I keep his fucking name straight.

"Yeah, Sammy. He hasn't really been around lately, which sucks. We are so close, but also trying to juggle school and all. You know?" Sammy. Her little name for him cracks me up.

"I get it."

She looks up at me and smiles. It's like she knows me—like she sees me. "I probably shouldn't have texted you."

"Why?" I ask.

She shrugs, and my eyes fall to her collarbone. I'd love to lick up it, my hands wrapped around her...

"I mean, it's hard. He's never really had many friends and then he starts here and I see him with people all the time now. It's good for him, but I worry I'm losing him. Does that make sense?"

I tear my gaze away from her throat and look into her eyes. "Perfect sense, Sab."

She smiles again, and I feel like I won a prize. I'm going to be the best boyfriend ever to her. "Enough about me," she says.

"I like talking about you." I reach out to take a lock of her hair before letting it fall between my fingertips.

She nudges me playfully. "You're such a good listener." She bats her eyelashes at me. "I hope I didn't pull you away from anything important just to hear me rant." Her face scrunches up in the cutest way. Taking my hand off hers, I can't help but caress the apple of her cheek, the sun kissing it an alluring pink.

"Nothing is more important than you, Sab." Her eyes twinkle. "I'm serious. Call me anytime."

"Are we still on for dinner this weekend?" She starts to put her book in her bag, and I stand.

"Of course." I wouldn't miss it. That's the night we're going to get closer. I feel it.

"Good. I can repay you for listening to me ramble." She looks at her watch, then back to me. "I'm sorry, I need to get to my next class."

She waves her delicate little fingers at me in goodbye, her smile lighting up her whole face, before turning and heading back toward campus.

My dick is throbbing, and my balls ache. Fuck, there's something about that innocence I want to set on fire and dance in.

My phone chimes, and upon pulling it out, I can't help but hope it's Sab writing me some cute little message. But it's not her.

It's from Lillian.

"Counselor?" I smirk as I enter Lillian's office and slump my ass in her chair.

"Envy," she says, completely void of expression.

My mouth opens and closes like a goddamn fish.

Waving her hand in the air and rolling her eyes, she sits down on the corner of her desk and watches me. I don't say anything, waiting her out.

"I'm thinking we don't need to play the role of counselor and needy student anymore. No pretense considering how you ended up on the list of candidates. Poor Oliver, seems he met the devil."

She's rendered me fucking speechless. I feel like I'm made of stone right now.

"You and I could be good for each other."

My brow quirks, and she rolls her eyes. "Get your mind out of the gutter. I have others seeing to those needs. No, you can be useful in other areas."

"Like what?"

Standing, she rounds her desk and picks up a card, tapping it against the wood.

"This is your task. I'll be giving this to Pride, but I want to make it clear to you I need this task complete. No trading coins or bitching out of it. Serve me well, and you'll prosper far within The Elite while helping your brothers along the way. Piss me off, and I'll sink you faster than you could ever swim back to the surface."

Well, that's a fucking threat if I ever heard one.

"What is it?"

Licking her lips, she smiles. "It appears Rhett is wavering on his task. I want you to complete it for him."

Sitting forward, my brow furrows. "You mean Chastity?"

"Just get the video evidence of them together in a compromised position."

All this shit is fucked. Chastity is her step-kid.

"Why do you want this stuff?"

Folding her arms, her eyes squint. "That's none of your concern. Now, do what you're told and you remain Elite. Isn't that what you want?"

Fuck.

"Take this and get it done."

She pushes a small envelope over the table, then goes to her door, holding it open for me to leave.

When I get outside, I rip open the envelope, finding a note and cell phone.

Video the act and send to the only contact number in the contact list.

VII

UINCENDUM NATUS

THIRTEEN

I meet Pride at the nunnery later that night. The building is dark with just the whispering of the winds whisking across the ominous grounds. Pushing the wooden doors open, a lone candle sits in waiting, casting just enough light to illuminate Mason's face. Shadows lick his skin to where only his eyes, bridge of his nose, and lips can be seen.

"You ready?" He lowers his head. He's holding on to the piece of card I saw earlier today.

"Fuck yeah I'm ready." I take the card from him, and he rubs his hands together.

A sinister smile crawls across my face like a snake in the night as I read the task silently.

Envy is the art of taking on another's blessing instead of your own.

Brothers bond for life, so help your brother out.

ENVY

Keep his life Elite.
Video him with his task.
Take the choice from him.

I re-read it, knowing exactly what it means. Rhett had to record himself fucking the dean's daughter, but can't do it. He's fucking pussy-whipped. But he needs The Elite, and I'm a team player. I'll help him out.

I can. The Elite know my strengths. Lillian fucking knows my strengths.

"The coin given to you by The Elite offers—"

"I know how it works, man," I cut him off, remembering the speech the night we all met in this very same place. He nods silently and acts calm while my chest hammers harder than ever before. A loathsome emotion dawns on me. I have to stab a brother in the back to complete my task. Growing a close bond with The Elite is something I pride myself on. What if Rhett finds out I'm the one responsible for documenting the sin between him and the dean's daughter and wants revenge?

I close the card, my emotions conflicted. Fuck. It's like I'm growing fucking feelings or something.

I *have* to take over Rhett's task, though. The Elite needs him, and in his time of despair, he cannot rise.

"You good?" Mason asks, sensing my unease.

I smile, masking my uncertainty.

"Never better."

"So, you're able to do your task?"

Rubbing my chin, I think about where Rhett is staying so I can get his schedule down. Shit, how do I get to him without a car? Fuck, I could have someone take me, but I'd rather stalk alone. Plus, if I take a brother with me, they might not like my task and spill the whole thing to Rhett.

Even if this is for his own good, I don't want to risk losing the brotherhood. I've never really had guys like this to back me up—to sling a beer back and shoot the shit. You need good company if you're going to be successful at anything. So, I've got to play both cards, pleasing The Elite and my brothers. I'll make do without a car for now, but I'm going to need one in the long run—and Lillian did say if I needed anything to ask.

"I'm going need a ride, a car of my own," I state, more to myself than him.

"I can make that happen," Pride informs me. "Until then, you can borrow my car to get your task done."

My eyes snap to his. That's right, I'm in The Elite. "Thanks, brother."

I pull out my cell and shoot a text to all brothers.

Me: What's everyone up to?

Everyone replies about another bullshit party going on at God's, this time at his apartment. Apparently the last one was at his parents' house. I can give a fuck, but then Rhett adds he'll be there with Chastity.

Bingo.

Guess a party's in order after all.

When Mason and I walk into God's ritzy as fuck party, the music hits me, along with a few college girls who scream, *spank me, I have daddy issues*. I'm tempted to take a few in an open room and show them just who their daddy is, but my eyes fall on Samuel in the corner slamming on his phone. I wonder if he's talking to Sabella. Does he know about us? Would he wrap his own hands around my neck and squeeze until my last breath is choked from my lips knowing her and I are meant to be?

I walk over, my casual charade in place, and throw my

arm around his shoulder. "Sammy, what's the frown for? Someone denying the Gunner monster cock?" I laugh, and he shrugs my arm off.

"No. It's my sister, Sabella. She's always on my ass about getting my life together." *Sabella.* The way he says her name with annoyance brings a boil to my blood. She should be spoken about with adoration. Beauty. When she becomes mine, I'll never let a single motherfucker talk ill of her like that. Even her fucking *twin* brother. My chest starts to tighten, and my vision blurs a bit. Fuck, the beast inside wants to come out and destroy. Who gives a shit if he's my brother. *She's* about to be my everything.

"Anyway, what's up? Did you just meet with Mason?" He finishes off his text and looks up at me. I don't mask my anger quick enough, and he sees the building hatred in my eyes. "What the fuck's that look for?"

If I don't check myself, he'll find out. In and out, I breathe. *Calm the fuck down.* Sammy's my brother. I need to keep my cool.

God walks up, breaking the tension. "You bitches wanna party?" he asks, grinding his teeth.

I'm never one to turn down a good time, and right now, a jolt of blow would do me some good. I nod and slap Samuel on the back. "Just what the doctor ordered." I throw my signature Joker smile across my face. "Sorry, Sammy. Raincheck on this heart to heart. Got an appointment."

I walk away and into a room, shoving my nose into a mountain of cocaine.

When I resurface, Samuel is nowhere in sight. Fuck, neither is Rhett and his little blonde bombshell. I whip out my phone and shoot a text to Rhett asking where the fuck he went. He doesn't reply. Fuck. I just want this task done.

It's four a.m. when a message comes in from Rhett.

Lust: Sorry, bro, my girl needed to be home.

Me: You wanna do something tonight?

Lust: Taking Chastity to the carnival.

Rubbing my chin, I vaguely remember seeing flyers about the carnival in town. My face is numb as fuck, but I still feel my smile spread wide across my face. With both of them being there, I can check them out better, get a feel of what's happening between them, and hopefully get this shit done. Perfect.

Me: Snooze fest. Have fun.

Lust: Oh, I will.

Good. That's what I'm hoping.

I've waited all day for nightfall, preparing for my task. Wearing my favorite black hoodie and black pants to conceal my identity, I stay near the back of the lingering crowds at the carnival. Women wearing tank tops and shorts that barely cover their asses stomp by without so much as a glance in my direction. I could easily wrap my hand around their mouths and take them from the scene without anyone knowing. Strollers with sticky, grubby kids crying for more of something pass by. The sound of rides clanking and chugging makes me nervous one is about to drill into me at any second. The smell of deep fried foods and sugary goodness has my belly growling, but I don't have time for pleasure. I'm here for business.

My eyes sweep across unknown faces, looking for Rhett and Chastity.

I doubt anything juicy will happen here, but afterward, there's gotta be some fireworks at her or Rhett's place. I will follow, record, and complete my task.

My chest vibrates with unfamiliar warmth. I feel guilty for doing this to Rhett, for cutting into his privacy like this, but it needs to be done. An act of tough love. The Elite needs this documentation for some reason, and me doing this for Rhett will get just that while securing Rhett's place in The Elite.

The crowd starts to whistle and clap, getting hyped over something, which grabs my attention. There they are. Rhett's kissing her like nobody's watching, her eyes closed and dress drifting around her knees. Who knew Rhett could be a romantic little fucker. I swallow the jealously stuck in my throat. I can't help but wish it was Sab and I. To have everyone cheering us on, wanting us to love one another. We could be lost in our own circle, riding on the high of love. It makes no sense to me why I can't keep a woman by my side. It amazes me how a woman can drop you from their existence after you've given them everything.

Rhett and Chastity begin to move, and so do my thoughts. I have to stay focused. This is about them. Not me and Sab.

Treading slowly, I move around the hot dog stand, the smell of blistered pork overriding the sugary floss. I keep my eyes on the couple. Jesus, they can't keep their fucking hands off each other. They really do enjoy each other's company. Could even love one another, sacrifice for one another. How does Rhett do it? How does he accept her flaws and feel for her? How does she love him so much?

My aching feet have me stepping side to side, trying to ease the pain, the sweat dripping down my back, making me itch. I've followed Rhett and Chastity all night. They've been on every fucking ride already and hit every food stand. What more do they have to do? *Come on, let's leave!*

Chastity carries a big pink bear, looking at Rhett with goo-goo eyes, and I start to become impatient. Kneeling down, I pluck up a rock and watch them, bored.

"Tell him you're ready to go home and fuck his brains out," I whisper to myself.

They turn toward the mirror house. Shit, if they go in there, I won't be able to see them. Rubbing my chin, I think about if Sab and I went into a mirror house. I wouldn't be able to keep my hands off her. We'd dart behind scratched glass where nobody could see us, copping a feel until I fucked her senseless.

Yeah, I need to get in there. If they do anything tonight, it's got to be in there.

Just as Rhett and Chastity hand in their tickets to go inside, I make quick work of getting behind the attraction. Finding a door unlocked, I open it and slide right in.

It's dark, stuffy, and the sound of my weight on the weak floor beneath me sounds as if I'm about to fall right through. Now I see why my mother never let me go into these things as a kid. It wasn't because we were poor, but because they are really dangerous.

Giggles sound through the wall, and I quietly step up to the black wall. A small hole is lit up, inviting me to look through it.

Rhett and Chastity are on the other side, the pink bear now lying on the ground and Chastity practically crawling up Rhett like a fucking tree. Rhett falls to his knees, pushing her dress up eagerly before her dainty panties fall to her ankles. I can't help but focus on the patch of blonde hair right between her thighs. Fuck, I wanna be closer to that pussy. Is she wet? Tight?

My dick pulses, aching to be in Rhett's place right now. Only…I want Sab panting for me to please her. Taking out the phone I was given for the task, I click record and watch the screen capture it all.

He puts one of her feet on his shoulder, opening her thighs up for him. They're whispering to each other, but I can't tell what they're saying over my own heavy breathing.

Just like that, his face is deep in her pussy. The sound of him lapping and sucking her juices has me shifting my dick. She withers beneath him, her body trembling with pleasure.

His head tilted just right, he keeps his eyes on her as he slips a finger deep inside, causing her to nearly buckle at the knees. Biting my lip, I feel a bead of cum slipping from my own dick. God, I'd do anything to grab her face and make her look me in the eyes while I ate that pretty pussy.

When she comes, I nearly fall against the rickety wall with my own release. My eyes close as I pant, trying to get my shit together. Fuck, I'm so goddamn horny now.

I grip the phone tightly. I did it. I completed my task.

Stepping outside, I take a deep breath and pull the hood off my head, my legs feeling like dead weights after that intense adrenaline rush. Sweat beads down the side of my face, my chest as heavy as my dick.

UINCENDUM NATUS

FOURTEEN

Waking up the next morning, it's fucking loud. Too loud for… I look for my watch to see what time it is. The blinding sun whisks through the blinds from the window, causing me to wince. Someone is playing music. Shit music. I have every thought of finding who it is and strangling them with their speaker cord.

Throwing my legs over the bed, I yawn and scratch at my stomach. Reaching for my phone, I check to see if the boys or Sab have messaged me.

Sab texted me two hours ago.

Sab: Looking forward to tomorrow night's dinner!

I reply. **Me: Me too, beautiful.**

It's not lost on me that I'd never say the words to anyone. Is it because I really like her, or am I just playing the game?

ENVY

Thinking of Sab makes my mind drift to my brothers. Most of all, Rhett. My task. I had to fuck him over, but it was for his own good. He doesn't want to be out of The Elite. I know he doesn't. Rubbing my hands up and down my face, I push my lazy ass off the bed. I sit down at my computer chair and pull the phone over to me. Opening my text messages, I hit the send button to the contacts instructed by Lillian and the send a text to Pride.

Me: Task is done.

I don't care who needs it or wants it. My task is done. I mean, it's not like Rhett and Chastity fucked. I'm really doing him a favor in getting this. It could be much worse. We're the guys who play God without permission, after all.

I need an energy drink. A big ass Red Bull with a muffin.

My stomach growls thinking about it.

Getting dressed in some jeans and a button-up, I pull the sleeves up to my elbows. It's supposed to rain today, so I grab a jacket.

Getting the rest of my shit together, I head out of my room, shoving through the group of kids singing along to some stupid fucking song I've never heard. They give me a hateful look, but I don't give a fuck.

Some frizzy, curly-haired chick with a dress sweeping down to her ankles, hiding any figure she might have, comes strutting toward me like she's on a mission.

"Good morning! Take one and—"

"No," I bite out, the tone of my voice as sharp as a shard of glass. The girl swallows, pulling the vibrant pink piece of paper to her chest.

"Well, okay then."

I have to get a place of my own. I can't handle this frat party shit anymore. Running my hand through my hair, I press past the terrified girl, the look on my face alone keeping anyone else from bothering me.

Shoving the door open with a little too much animosity, I gasp for fresh air.

"You look like shit," Mason observes. My eyes slowly rise from my shoes to the amused eyes of my brother, Pride. Was he waiting for me?

"I gotta get out of the dorms, brother. I can't handle this shit anymore," I explain, exhausted.

He glances up at the building before displaying a pair of keys, the keyring stuck to his thumb.

I raise a brow, and he gestures them toward me, a smile on his face.

"Well, you going to take them?"

"They're for me?" I ask, a little stunned.

"Yeah." He chuckles. Stepping forward, I take the keys, the feeling of them in my palm exhilarating.

"What do they go to?"

"You asked for a car, didn't you? Apparently, your wish is The Elite's demand."

My face sobers, an expression of "you're fucking kidding" taking over.

"I can't believe how fast you got your task done. The Elite must have been confident with you, huh?" He runs his hands along the back of his neck, rubbing it as if he's anxious. I bet being in charge of six fucking men is tiring.

"Get your task done and many things will come."

I chuckle.

He pulls his attention from our conversation to something that just came through on his phone. My stomach drops. The video I took. He's about to know what I did.

"Hey, you all right, man?" I question.

My nerves are on high alert, and I'm ready to fight. To kill. I did what I had to do. What *everyone* will have to do to join The Elite. Lie, cheat, deface.

His eyes snap to mine.

"Yeah. Fine." The strain wrinkling the sides of his eyes tells me otherwise. "Just got another task to hand out. Let me know if you need anything else. Yeah?"

"Consider it done," I murmur, but he's already walking away. So it wasn't the video. Damn, I'm going to be on edge every damn day being part of this brotherhood.

Relief washes through me. I release the painful breath I was holding and start toward the west quad parking lot. "He seems to live another day." I chuckle to myself.

"She's parked over there!" Mason yells over his shoulder, pointing toward the front of campus. My eyes follow his finger to a brand new looking black Audi. Holy shit! This day is starting to take a turn in my favor.

Time to take my brothers for a ride, starting with Micah.

Pulling my phone out, I shoot him a text.

Me: Wanna take my new car for a joy ride?

Greed: Can't. Meeting Mason.

Opening the door to my new car, the smell of leather nearly gives me a fucking boner. Slipping into her, I grab the steering wheel, getting acquainted with her. Glancing along the knobs and dials, I find a folded note, one that resembles The Elite.

Welcome to The Elite.

"Holy shit I did it," I mutter to myself.

Feeling accomplished, I pull Sabella's name up,

needing to have her this second.

Me: Where are you?

Sabella: Home, why?

Me: Sam home?

Sabella: No...

Me: I'm coming over!

We're about to see how fast she goes tonight as I rush to my sweet Sabella.

UINCENDUM NATUS

FIFTEEN

Pulling up to a large, colonial-style house, the gate opens before I even have to stop and buzz myself in.

She's been waiting for me.

It's dark because of the nasty storm brewing, so I can't see much detail, but I pull into a circular drive and turn my car off. I slide out of the car with determination and ease. The large oak door to their house opens, and there stands my Sabella in waiting. She's wearing a pink cami with gray sweats, her hair piled on top of her head.

I smile. She always makes me smile.

"Well, look what the devil dragged in," she teases.

But all I can think about is how Sabella and I would make the perfect fairytale.

Ahhh. Once upon a time, an angel fell in love with a devil—it ended in chaos.

"I needed to see you," I explain, walking up to her.

"Is that right?" Her voice holds a hint of glee, which excites me. She wanted to see me too.

Wrapping my arms around her, I pull her close. She's so tiny, and the smell of her fresh-showered skin and clean clothes makes me want to hang on tighter.

"Wow," she murmurs, trying to pull free from my death grip, and I'm suddenly aware she's not completely mine. A cold vast spreads throughout my chest at the thought of me losing her. It scares me. I want everything Sab has to offer. I want her to open up to me, bare her soul and be mine for all eternity. She's so pure and happy. I need her in my life.

"Do you want a drink or something?" She clears her throat, and I sense she's uncomfortable.

"A drink would be great." I tuck a lock of hair behind her ear. It's so silky and soft. It feels like a spool of silk. She's so beautiful.

Turning on her bare heel, she heads to what I presume is the kitchen. Once inside, I'm in a large foyer, a grand staircase making its way up to the second floor. The place is huge, maybe even bigger than my uncle's home.

"I have water, milk..." she calls from the other room. One foot in front of the other, I follow her voice. She's in the kitchen with the fridge door open, one leg bent and resting on her big toe as she gazes through the shelves.

"Water will be fine."

She reaches forward, grasping a bottle, and tosses it my way. I catch it.

"So, why did you want to see me so bad? Everything okay?"

Unscrewing the cap, I take a big swig, my eyes eating

in every inch Sab has to offer.

Cool water splashes down my throat, but it does nothing to snuff out the desire burning in my chest.

Placing the water on the counter, I saunter over to her, taking in her supple curves and the roundness of her heavy breasts. God, what I'd do to suck on one of those tits.

Her mouth parts, her eyes glazing over like fog casting across the lands on an early morning.

I grip her hips, pull her up, and set her on top of the marble counter. Pushing myself between her legs, I grasp the back of her neck and tug her mouth to mine.

She kisses me back, the softest lips I've ever come into contact with moving against my own. It's passionate, filled with urgency and deep meaning. I cup her face with both of my hands, then peck her once before I pull away.

"Open your eyes, Sabella," I demand softly. She does, gray irises saturating my soul in love and fear. I kiss her once, twice, and one more time, holding her gaze.

"Trust me?" I ask.

My dick throbs as if someone slammed it in a door. I need to be between her legs, soaking up her heat.

I trace her collarbone, and she tenses, but doesn't tell me to stop, so I go lower, pushing her top to the side and slipping my palm up her stomach. Fuck, she's so creamy soft. Resting my head against her forehead, I can feel her heavy breaths, the sound of her thoughts nearly outdoing my own.

My thumb brushes against the swell of her breast, and she freezes at the contact.

"Wait!" She grips me by the wrist, pushing my hand down and away from her. "I don't want to do this. I'm not ready," she whispers, shaking her head.

Disappointment fills my chest, my hard-as-fuck cock nearly ready to explode in my pants.

Taking a step back, I run my hand over my face. It's hot. I'm suddenly fucking hot.

"Are you mad?" She frowns, pulling her clothes back in place and wiping her mouth.

I shake my head no, but I am. I'm so upset. I want Sabella to love me. I want her to be so overfilled with urgency and desire, she can't keep her hands off me.

Like Sam and Patience.

Rhett and Chastity.

When am I ever going to have that kind of love, that feeling of being needed—wanted?

"Sam might come home any minute," she murmurs, awkwardness filling the room. She wants me to leave. Fuck.

"Yeah. I better be going." I turn, unable to look at her.

"Are you still coming over for dinner?" The happy note in her voice lights a little hope inside that she still wants to be with me. Maybe she just needs to go at her own pace.

Smiling, I turn, but not all the way.

"Of course, Sab." I smile, but it's a façade. I was just fucking rejected. The sting is a little deep and not easily forgettable.

Escorting myself out of the house, I find my car and get in. Starting it, my hands nearly strangle the steering wheel. I'm hurt. I'm angry. I'm sad.

I've never had to chase a woman before, not to this extent. Never had to work so hard. Most women want to be with me, want to love me. It's me who can't love them—they weren't the ones—they always fucked it up in some way.

Go figure, I finally found *the one*, and she can't recip-rocate the emotion. As soon as I laid eyes on Sabella, I knew she was different, and I'm not going to let her get away from me that easily.

I move to tug my phone out, but find my pocket empty. I check the other pocket, but it's empty too. Fuck, I must have set my phone down inside Sabella's house. Getting out, I skip a few steps up to the front door of Sab's house and invite myself in. I'll be in and out.

"Sab?" I call out to her, letting her know I'm back. I hear her voice, but she's not talking to me.

"I don't know. He's super sweet, but I get this Ted Bundy feeling around him, you know?"

I pause. Sabella is talking to someone about me, oblivious I'm just around the corner.

"Yeah, he seems normal, but he's not. He's just… not. You have to be around him to feel what I feel, to understand the red flags. Still, I think he needs someone, a friend, and I'm not sure how I feel about that. He wants more than friendship, but what if that's all I can offer?"

My nostrils flare, more anger than ever before firing through my limbs. Snatching my phone off the counter by the bottle of water, I turn around and stomp out of the house.

Ted Bundy, really?

Getting in my car, I punch the steering wheel, scrap-ing the thin skin over my knuckles. How dare she portray me like that. Does she even know what I'll do for her? I'm going to give her everything. I slam my fist once more, my skin slicing open across my middle knuckle. Once she's mine, she'll learn not to use those hurtful words. Right now, I can't think about that.

I grab my phone and open that stupid fucking party app. I need to stick my dick in something, release some of these confused feelings I can't seem to push through right now. I just need to get Sab out of my fucking head for two goddamn seconds.

Of course God is having another party. Naturally, I chose to bond with my brothers for the night. If anyone gets me laid, it will be them.

Inside, there's a heavy pulse of music thudding through the apartment, smoke hugging the ceiling, and it's body-to-body packed with people.

"Sebastian!" Micah calls after me, his fist raised for a bump.

I pat his back, and he pulls me an arm's length away.

"You all right?" He senses my unease.

Jaw clenched, I shake my head.

"I just need to get laid."

He chuckles.

"My man, you came to the right place."

God places a cup of amber liquid in my hand, and Micah starts pointing out potential fucks for the night as if he's reading off a dinner menu. The music tunes out, the sound of my brothers' voices difficult to understand. I'm lost in this moment of brotherly bonding. I have people who care about me. That want me to be happy and are excited to see me. This is a first for me, and I'm not sure how to handle it.

I've never had that before. I smile, happily. I'm glad I decided to come here tonight. If I ever did anything right in my life, it was putting my name on The Elite's list.

Micah sits on the back of a couch, a cigarette hanging from his mouth, his eyes closed. I wanna nudge him and talk to him, but I decide pussy first. I need to let some of these feelings out.

Laughing at whatever Pride just said, I take a swig from my cup.

It's strong. Really fucking strong.

"Easy, brother. That's liquid gold!" Micah laughs. Coughing, I smile at him and take another swig. Getting fucked up is just what I need.

"Where is God? This is his party." I frown.

Shaking his head, Pride's hand around his glass almost shatters the damn thing.

"He went to talk Rhett off a ledge. He's fucked up over Chastity dumping him."

Thud. Thud. Thud.

Fuck!

I can't think about this shit. I need to get laid.

"Think I'm going to find some company, boys," I state, earning a bunch of pats on the back as I exit the room. It's not lost on me that neither of them want to come hunt with me.

Heading into the next room, sipping from my cup, I look over the girls in the house.

We've got the Barbies, the goths, the nerds.

My eyes land on a particular girl sitting on the counter like a delicate wallflower in the kitchen.

Her hair is brown, eyes gray like a little prude I know.

She looks similar to Sabella. If I can't have Sab, I might as well find the next best thing.

Smiling behind my cup, I head toward her. The skanky top showing half her tits is not something Sabella would wear, though. I find it unflattering on her.

With a lift of my chin, I say, "Hey." She smiles instantly. I hold my hand out to her.

"I'm Sebastian."

Hooded eyes slide up my frame. "I know who you are."

"You do?"

"Yeah, anyone who is friends with God is a friend of mine." She flips her hair over her shoulder.

Huh, so I have a reputation that precedes me. That's a first. Or is it?

"I'm Chancy," she informs.

"You look bored, Chancy." I try to push her into conversation. I don't want to chase her. I'm over that shit for the night.

Leaning back on her hands, her chest pushing her maybe B-cup breasts out, she licks her lips.

"I'm very...bored." She's fishing. Fishing for me to take her to a room. Perfect.

I lean into her personal space. She doesn't tense like Sabella, and she doesn't shrink back. She opens up like Chastity or Patience would for one of my brothers.

Running my finger down her chin, I focus on her lips. They're plump, but don't look as soft as Sabella's.

"I can help with that." My offer seductively slips from my lips in a low tone.

"Yeah?" she whispers, opening her legs to let me step between them. She's easy. I should like that considering

Sabella is being a fucking prude, but it turns me off. Beggars can't be choosers, though. I need pussy, and this girl is offering.

"Wanna go upstairs, beautiful?" My cock stands at attention, ready for action. I don't want to wine and dine, or whisper sweet nothings into…what's this chick's name again?

"I thought you'd never ask." She grins, the gray in her eyes holding secrets. I'm good at reading people, and it's obvious this girl is looking for human connection. Someone hurt her, or made her mad. She wants to revenge fuck, and I'm down for it.

So much for a wallflower.

My hips thrust into her, my hand wrapped into her hair and pulling until her back is arched enough for me to grasp a tit. She pants and moans as I give it to her from behind.

"Oh my God! Oh my God!" she cries out, her tone dancing the line of pain and pleasure. Closing my eyes, I envision Sabella on the other end of my dick. Her sweet giggles and soft body. The way her innocent eyes would look up to me as I corrupted her.

"Right there!" The chick's words cut through my vision, pissing me off.

"Shut up," I growl, losing my release.

I pinch her nipple, imagining Sabella's. So soft and perky. She'd moan for me to lick and suck it. To love her unconditionally.

"Yesss!"

Goddamn it, why won't this bitch shut up? I slap my hand around her mouth to shush her, and clench my eyes shut harder. Sabella. Think of Sabella.

I see her smile behind my eyes, her lashes fluttering against her flushed skin. Little pinpricks scatter up my arm, but I'm too close to care why. I feel her body thrashing beneath me, getting into it. *Yeah, move on my dick, Sabella. Grind, baby.*

My dick twitches with warning, and my hand tightens on the girl's hair. My sweet Sabella. Love me. Need me as much as I need you.

Just like that, I find my release, my body twitching with every last pump.

Opening my eyes, my dick deflates like a balloon at a kid's birthday party. This bitch is anything but my sweet Sabella. Her skin is flushed, her tit bruised, and she's as sweaty as a pubescent teenager. Bloody fingernail marks and scratches line both my arms, and tears flood the girls face. I remove my hand, and she slaps my face. "You bastard, I couldn't breathe," she sobs, almost tripping over herself to get away from me. She stumbles from the bed and lands with a thud.

I grab my jeans and start shoving my legs through them. This fuck did nothing for me. I'm still just as tense and uptight as I was before I fucking came to this party.

"I gotta go," I mumble.

"Yeah, go. You asshole." She sniffles, moving farther away from me as I round the bed. I hustle out of the room and hunt down another drink.

VII

UINCENDUM NATUS

SIXTEEN

I find myself outside Sabella's house half drunk. She sleeps with the window open, and I know for a fact she leaves the front door unlocked because Sammy boy might come home late.

I hate how irresponsible you are with your privacy, my sweet girl. Anyone could come in and put their hands on you, snoop around your things, or even take them.

Makes me want to strangle Sam for leaving her to her own devices. I open the front door, then quietly close it and skim the stairs to the room I presume is hers, the pink and white curtains dancing in the wind. My heart races to find her sleeping soundly in her sleigh canopy bed—*like a princess.*

Her room is spotless. Not even a tacky Jason Momoa poster hanging above a mirror splattered with empowering girl power quotes.

There's a small vanity on the wall adjacent from her bed, and a bookshelf and desk next to the window. I skim my fingertips over her things, stopping when I come into contact with her computer.

Opening her laptop, I run my fingers over the keys, and the screen comes to life. She was last on Facebook an hour ago. I scroll to her latest post.

#Livingmybestlife.

My lips pull up into a smirk. *My troubled girl. Who are you trying to convince?*

I come to a book laying next to her computer.

Pride and Prejudice. Interesting. *I pictured you as more of a tacky romance reader.* Picking it up, I can almost feel where her hands touched it before she decided to lay down and rest her beautiful, sad eyes. My gaze drifts to her sleeping form. She's lying on her stomach, a fluffy pillow snuggled up under her head. *So cute,* yet infuriating. *Being in here and seeing the real you—the one nobody gets to see—just makes me want you more.*

Setting the book down, I step over to her vanity, picking up the half-empty perfume bottle.

Mmm...it smells of fresh laundry—*like you.* I spray it on myself to get rid of the smell of the slut I just fucked.

She stirs in her sleep, making my adrenaline spike. Setting down the bottle, I move to her bedside and pull the blankets over her back to keep the wind billowing through the cracked window from biting at her delicate skin.

"Shhh," I whisper, petting her silky hair, and she settles, my voice calming her back into a dream. *See? You do need me, you just don't know it yet.*

"Sleep, my sweet Sabella. I'll see you tomorrow."

UINCENDUM NATUS

SEVENTEEN

'm woken up by the boys barging into my dorm room like a fucking marching band.

"Get your hands off your dick. Time to get up!" Rhett laughs, carrying an empty cardboard box.

It's good to see him laughing. Pride text me last night to let me know him and his girl sorted things out. God came to the rescue.

"What's going on?" I question, sitting up in my bed, making sure my blanket is covering my morning wood. The room fills with the smell of expensive cologne and the earthy tones of weed. That would be The Elite. My boys.

"You're getting your own place," Rush explains, throwing some of my crap into an unlabeled box.

"Really?" About fucking time.

"Yeah, The Elite said to get you moved in." Mason shrugs, revealing a key. I swear, he's like a fucking genie.

"First things first, party at your new place!" Sam grins like a teenage boy, his punk rocker looking jacket giving him the perfect bad boy image.

"How about tonight?" Rush, or Sloth, questions with a long drawl of his words.

They begin to chatter about booze and music, and all I can think about is how I'm going to turn them down because I'm supposed to have dinner with Sabella. I can't tell them either, because Sam will rip my fucking head off.

"I...uh, I can't tonight. Got plans with some girl I met." I try to explain as vaguely as I can.

"Met a girl, eh?" Rhett puts his hands on his hips, looking over the room for more shit to put in his box.

"Would it be Chancy? She's hit up my cell phone bitching about you getting rough, like I need to hear about that shit. I don't even know how she got my number." Rush chuckles. Just hearing that bitch's name makes me want to shower.

"No, it's not Chancy," I snap.

"I cannot believe The Elite is giving you a place to stay," Micah scoffs, moseying through my clothes.

"Me either," I murmur.

"What was your task?" God asks casually, and a pain strikes my chest. Oh fuck.

"Are we supposed to tell?" I raise a brow.

"Seems everyone knows what everyone's task has been," Rhett informs.

Running my hand back and forth through my hair, anxiety begins to trickle down my back in the form of sweat.

Tapping the side of my nose, I side-eye the boys, not saying a word. I'll never tell.

"You're one creepy fucker, you know that?" Rhett chuckles, but I can tell he's serious. Smiling, I look him in the eye, conveying just how uncomfortable this can get.

"Well, we don't need Sebastian to throw the party." Sam laughs, making the rest of the guys chuckle.

"True! I mean, I am fucking moving your shit out of the goodness of my heart." Micah raises a brow, standing at the back of the group.

I really don't want to miss out on a party, but I can't call Sabella and tell her I'm bailing on dinner for my boys. Any other girl, I would, but I can't with her, not after she wants to friendzone me. I need to work on her, show her how perfect we can be together. I wish I could just bring her with me. Sam has to find out about us at some point.

"Hey, you want this creepy ass black hoodie to go too?" Micah asks me, looking through my clothes to pack. That's the shit I wear when I'm stalking or deeply investigating someone. It's my favorite.

"Nah, I only wear that when I'm stalking your mom," I tease, but the irony is if I knew where his mom lived, I probably would be outside her window.

He flips me off, not taking me seriously.

My phone beeps, and I swipe it off the desk before Sam can.

Sab: **My dad is home, can we reschedule dinner?**

I want to be mad, because I really wanted to see her, but that actually works perfectly. It also occurs to me if she doesn't want her dad to know about me yet, then she sure as hell doesn't want Sam to. This makes me want her more for some reason—like a challenge to get into her inner circle of trust.

Me: How about my place tomorrow night? I offer.

Sabella: Your place?

Me: Yeah. I'm moving out of the dorms today.

Sab: Sounds perfect!

"Is that the girl who's got you pussy-whipped?" Micah questions, and I quickly lock my screen before anyone can see her name.

"She had to reschedule. Looks like we can have that party, after all." Rubbing my hands together, I stand, my dick at full attention. I usually have to jerk it to get it to go down when it's this fucking hard. Son of a bitch is throbbing like a finger stuck in a door.

"Jesus Christ, who have you killed with that thing?" Rhett tries to look away, but the size of my dick has him in shock.

Hands on my hips, I present it proudly.

"No one. Yet." I shrug, serious.

Dressed and in my car, I follow Mason to my new residence. Just a few blocks away from campus, he pulls alongside a curb and turns his car off. Looking to the right, I find a two-story house. The top floor is mostly glass, and the bottom is brick with black trimmings.

"It's nice," Micah observes.

"Any place is better than that fucking dorm," I growl, turning my engine off.

Getting out, Mason throws his arms out on each side and begins to walk backwards.

"Home fucking sweet home!" he show tunes.

Heading up to the front door, it has a security box.

"Do you know the code?" I jut my chin at the white box next to the door.

"Fuck no." Mason lifts the cover, observing it.

"Try six-six-six." Micah chuckles.

I press 666, and it beeps before unlocking the door.

"We have one of these, but it's hardly ever set," Sam states to nobody in particular, reminding me of how I just walked into their house last night. It's funny how people think that unknown evils lurk at night, but it's the ones that blend in during the light of day you should really be worried about.

Me.

Mason pushes the door open, the smell of new paint and flooring greeting us. Stairs lead to the second floor right when you walk in. The kitchen to the left, living room to the right.

It's on the smaller side, but the entire place is furnished.

Leather furniture, granite tops with appliances and cutting boards. The contemporary style is right up my alley.

Sell your soul and you'll get the best house on the block.

"I gotta take a piss," Sam informs, stepping around us in search of the bathroom.

I head up the stairs. The master bedroom has floor-to-ceiling windows. A giant king-sized bed with white blankets that resemble fucking clouds claiming the mattress. Candles and other knickknacks on the dresser in front of it. It's luxurious.

Stepping into the bathroom, the tub is invitingly massive. I could fit four people easily.

"Better get some curtains before you start fucking," Micah says from behind me, looking in over my shoulder at my room. He's right. Everyone in the neighborhood will know every pubic hair on and around my dick before the end of the week.

"That takes the fun out of everything." I grin.

He chuckles, and we both turn around and head downstairs to get my shit.

"This place is more like a home. I'm not feeling the party vibe here," Rush states from kitchen, his hand sliding back and forth over the granite top in admiration.

"He's got a point." God chuckles.

"Let's just go to your place then. I would rather your bed get used for fucking than mine." I toss my arm around his neck and pull him close. "Unless you want to slip into my bed and make it real interesting." I wink. Making God feel uncomfortable is like a fucking high.

"I told you he was gay!" Sam yells from the other room.

"I love everyone, what can I say?" I smirk, fucking with God further, before he pulls out from underneath of me, making me laugh my ass off.

God was right. His place is much more suitable for parties. It's bigger, and everyone knows where it is. His apartment is packed within an hour, and I've already had way too much to drink. I'm feeling the line between guilty for betraying Rhett and doing his task for him, and horny. Sabella is on my mind, and I want her. Badly. So fucking badly.

Micah sits on the couch beside me, his head laid back

as he smokes a cigarette with one hand, a drink in the other. Rhett sits on the other side of the room, texting on his phone. Probably Chastity. I wish Sabella would text me, tell me what she's doing and how she misses me.

We'll get there. She…will get there.

"We should do something tonight," God says, taking a gulp of his drink, his demeanor taking on a place of boredom.

"I'm game," I say.

"Like what? What you got in mind?" Rhett asks, not taking his eyes off his phone in his hand.

"I dunno. What about…let's get some ink?" God shrugs his left shoulder.

"Tattoos?" This has Rhett's attention.

"Yeah, you guys completed your tasks, you can get The Elite symbol now," Micah informs.

"You complete your task Rhett?" I ask, knowing I had to do it for him.

"Apparently." His voice takes a dip.

"So, I guess it's tattoo time, brother!" I punch God's left arm, and he eyes me crazily.

"The Elite gives us the time and place for the tattoos. They're done with hidden ink that only shows under a black light," Rhett informs me.

"Oh, well, we can still get inked. What they don't know and all that." I wink.

"I know a guy. Let's do it." He stands, stretching his arms out above his head.

"What about the party?" I ask, unsure of him leaving his place unattended.

"Nah. It'll be fine." He sips the rest of his drink, finishing it off.

Chuckling, we all file out of the house, "Where's Sam?"

"He got some shitty news earlier." Pride grunts.

They don't know it yet, but Sam and I are going to be closer than The Elite one day—especially after I make his sister fall in love with me.

I think back to the meeting I had with the devious Lillian today.

"Your brothers are proving a real disappointment." She croons, flicking invisible lint from her skintight pants.

"Is that so?" I smirk.

"How close are you with Samuel, Wrath?" Before I can answer, she bites her lip, then adds, "I know you have a thing for his sister."

This makes me straighten in my chair. "How the fuck would you know that?"

"You're not the only one who likes to dig around in people's business. Now, listen carefully. Wrath has been given a new task, and it involves his sweet, innocent sister."

Standing, I clench my fists. "What the fuck did you do?"

"It's not about what I do, it's what you do now. Convince Samuel to replace his sister with his lover, Patience. She can perform the task in Sabella's place."

"What do you want her to do?"

"She will seduce the dean."

"Your husband?"

"That doesn't concern you! Now, if you like your car, your apartment and status, and want your virginal little Sabella to remain that way, convince Samuel he needs to use Patience instead."

VII

UINCENDUM NATUS

EIGHTEEN

y bare chest is sprawled on a cold leather chair, a needle dipping in and out of my flesh. Thunder from some hardcore rock song vibrates through the speakers located in each corner of the studio. When God said he knew someone, I didn't see the guy doing my ink in mind. He looks like he belongs on *Ripley's Believe It or Not* with all his tattoos and piercings. He has a fucking dinner plate in his bottom lip for Christ's sake.

"How ya doing over there, brother?" God calls out from the chair beside me.

"Good," I reply, actually liking the sting behind the tattoo gun. The artist, Flash, wipes the area and continues.

Re-adjusting my chin on my hands, I look at Micah as he watches Flash work.

"Have you gotten your task yet, Micah?" His eyes slide

to mine, but quickly go back to the needle tickling my back. I smile. If he did, it's one he's not proud of—and if he hasn't, he ain't telling. We are a lot alike in many ways.

"All right, man. You're fucking done!" Flash's dopey tone alerts me, and I turn my neck, trying to look over my shoulder at the piece inflaming my back. Sitting up, he hands me a mirror to reflect off the back wall mirror so I can see the whole tattoo.

It's big, taking up my whole back. The majestic skull wearing a crown.

"I am The Elite," I murmur to myself. It feels so real now having it ingrained into my flesh, my blood mixing with the emblem of my family.

"Fucking A!" Micah clasps my hand in a brotherly way, pulling us close. I wasn't even aware he was done, or listening to me.

"It looks fucking good!" God nods, standing from his chair, looking at my huge ass tattoo. He went smaller, but go big or go home, right?

"It's on the house," Flash tells us, already beginning to clean up his work station.

"What?" I frown. Surely we owe something. We've been sitting here for hours.

"You heard me. It's covered." He shrugs a shoulder, not making eye contact.

God chuckles, scratching his chest.

"Fucking Elite, man!"

Wow, this is insane. Is this how it's going to be for the rest of my life, a road paved of free shit and respect? I mean, I had whatever my heart desired before because of my parents, but it came at the cost of lectures and threats. This...this is all mine.

Lifting my shoulders, my nostrils flare as a sudden empowerment and responsibility drive through my system.

"Fucking Elite."

My phone lights up with a text from Rush.

Sloth: I'm outside. Sam needs us at his mother's grave.

It's time to convince him to use his girl instead of mine.

Laying in my new bed, the blankets the softest I've ever fucking felt before, the screen of my phone illuminates across my face.

Me: You up? I text to Sabella.

Sab: Yeah, studying. What are you doing?

Me: Thinking of you.

I smile, because it's true.

Sab: Why are you so sweet?

Me: I'm not, trust me.

It takes her ages to reply, the little texting dots showing me she's writing, then deleting. Finally, her text comes through.

Sab: What do you want to eat tomorrow?

I wanna say "you," but that's too much for her. Though, I wonder if it would make her shimmy in place, adjust her wet panties.

Me: I'm up for anything. I just want to see you.

Sab: Why do you wanna see me so badly?

Tilting my head to the side, I bite at my lip in thought. There are a million reasons I want to see her, but what would she want to hear?

Me: You make me a better version of myself. I actually have something to look forward to each day.

That sounds cheesy as fuck, but it's true.

Three dots pop up, then disappear. I have the advantage here. I've left her speechless. Maybe hanging around Sam and Rhett lately has rubbed off on me. A true fucking Romeo coming out tonight, ladies and gentlemen.

I can't help but test the waters to see if my theory is true. Am I winning her over?

Me: What are you wearing?

Sab: What are you wearing? *silly face*

I chuckle, my dick growing at the mystery behind this woman. I can't figure out what makes her tick. I never know how she's going to react.

Me: I'm in bed, just my boxers. Now, you.

Seconds go by that feel like minutes. I begin to worry I've pushed her away, become too forward with my advances.

Then, a picture comes through, and I'm grabbing my aching cock before I even have a chance to look it over.

Fisting myself, my eyes feast on the beautiful Sabella. Her hair is messy, as if she's been running her fingers through it in frustration. A large St. Augustine shirt falls to her milky thighs. I can see just a glimpse of lacey white panties between her crossed legs, but fuck, not enough.

Her eyes are hooded, her lips swollen, like she's been biting them since I've been texting her.

Me: You look incredible. You should stay over tonight.

I need her, right fucking now, in this bed beside me. I wanna hold her, fall asleep next to her smelling her hair.

Sab: Easy, cowboy. I look like I've been studying all night because I have, and I'm tired. I'll see you tomorrow. Goodnight, Sebastian.

Wait, no.

Me: Come on, baby...
Sab: Night, Sebastian.

On that note, I swipe back up to her picture and enlarge it.

Pulling my cock out of my briefs, I pump it, pre-cum lubricating the sensitive skin.

I want to nip on her neck and hear her moan my name. My hand would slide up her shirt and grab her heavy breasts. I'd dip my head and nip at the rosebud of her nipple, sucking her skin into my mouth.

My hand swirls over the head of my dick, my entire cock vibrating with pressure. I need more wetness. Sabella's pussy would be as wet as a lake if she were with me. Pulling my palm up for a brief second, I spit on it and return it to my length for some relief.

Fuck yeah, that's better.

My hand slides up and down, pulling and tugging at the sensitive skin. My hips jerk up off the bed to the rhythm of my palm.

Sabella's eyes pierce into mine from the screen, my innocent girl turning into my bad little girl.

Those lips...I imagine them around my cock, sucking with an amateur force, but fuck, she does it so well.

Spurts of release suddenly blast through my palm and over my knuckles.

Groaning, I close my eyes and wish with every fucking beat of my heart it was Sabella and not my fucking hand until I ride the wave of ecstasy to the very end.

"Fuck," I whisper to the dark. Is this what love is? Sacrificing fucking a real person for your hand? Monogamy?

She'll be worth it.

She's special.

Different.

VII

UINCENDUM NATUS

NINETEEN

S tepping onto campus today, the wind blows a different direction, causing the hairs on the back of my neck to stand. It's going to be a crazy fucking day. I can tell.

The worry is short lived when I see Sabella coming my way, a big smile on her face. She's gorgeous. A white dress with a black belt hugs her waist, and she has on black flats to match.

"Hey, you!" I grab her by the hip and bring her closer to me. God, to feel her against me like this is a sedation to my overwhelming insecurities.

She hugs me, and quickly looks over her shoulder. For Sam, I know. He's really starting to get in the way of Sabella and I. I'll have to do something about this if it keeps happening. Maybe another accident like Olly—no, I can't do that to my brother. But if need be...

"I'll be at your place after my third class today." She pokes my chest, making me chuckle.

"I can't wait. I'll text you the address. Bring overnight clothes, yeah?"

Her cheeks redden, her shoulders tensing.

"If you want," I add, not wanting to make her feel like she doesn't have a choice in the matter.

"We'll see." She loosens up. "See you tonight!" Lifting up on her toes, she plasters a chaste kiss on my cheek and rushes off behind me.

Fuck, she does things to me.

Adjusting my bag on my shoulder, I head to my class for the morning, thoughts of Sabella still on my mind.

I notice Samuel stalking the grounds, his head down, and hands shoved into his jacket. He looks more pissed than usual.

"Yo!" I wave Sam down. He glances up, but waves me off. Something must really be off. Did he see Sabella and I? I roll my hand into a fist, ready to defend myself, but when he gets closer, he stops and shakes his head, as if something deeper is bothering him.

"What's up? How did things go with Patience?"

He doesn't answer.

"You all right?" I question him again.

"Just shit I gotta deal with," he grumbles. "I've gotta go."

"Wait, brother!" I stop him by grabbing his shoulder. I expect him to try to hit me, but he doesn't. His jaw ticks, his eyes focused ahead.

"Yeah, it's Patience. I like her, and my task is getting in the way of that." He rubs his hand over his face anxiously.

"It's nothing I can't handle. See you around."

What the fuck is going on? It seems the whole Elite has been shaken by the hands of the devil.

I guess the question is, can we handle the rock?

I find God at his apartment, sitting on a couch, lost in his own world. His elbows rest on his bouncing knees, his hands cupping his chin.

"Aren't you missing class?" he asks as I walk into the room, not even looking up.

"Heard one of our boys is in trouble," I exasperate, sitting down on a cushioned chair next to him.

He leans back. His elbow on the side of the chair, he rubs at his chin, side-eyeing me. He doesn't say a word. The silence does the speaking. Does he know it was me?

"When isn't there?" He grunts.

"Yeah, tell me about it. Glad things worked out for Rhett, though," I push, just wanting to know what he knows—if anything.

"Just covering up some shit that needs to be covered. Brotherhood is brotherhood. If it takes me taking the fall to smooth shit over, so be it." His words are cut-throat and to the point. "So, who's in trouble now?" he asks, his knee bouncing.

"Sam handed in his coin for another task." Shaking my head, I run my hands over my face, stressed. He better not change his mind. I won't allow Sab to be used by anyone.

Trying to clear the jumbled thoughts in my head, I

stand and pat God on the shoulder.

"See ya around, brother." I leave before things take a higher note. I know he needs his space, and I need mine, to be honest. Besides, I need to stay focused. I have an important date tonight with Sabella. Everything in me is riding on the evening to come.

VII

UINCENDUM NATUS

TWENTY

S tanding in my kitchen, I stare at the lone rose in the vase. The thorns pierce sharp, laddering up to a blossoming crimson beauty. Cupping the flower, I twirl it in my palm. My first rose to give to someone. I want to tell my uncle about it, but fuck him. He hasn't even called to check on me since he gave me his ultimatum. Not that I need him.

"It conveys something you cannot say, but feel." His voice echoes through my head as visions of him thrusting into his mistress, her teeth bearing down on the sharp stem, come to mind.

Love, what a stupid, mysterious thing you are.

You win some, you lose some. Except for me. I always win, and I will have Sabella.

I refuse to feel the sting of defeat.

Checking my watch again, I get irritated she's late. I type out a message, but then delete it. If her brother sees it, she may not make it here at all.

That fucker is becoming a problem.

Turning to the wall behind me, I fiddle with the stereo system. It's complicated. Every time I turn the dial left, it blares a song I could care less about listening to.

Lights flash through the windows, and I stand up tall, my heart beating faster. I feel like a teenage kid stalking my first girlfriend all over again. I decide to turn the stereo down and deal with it later.

Heading to my front door to let her in, I watch her struggle with getting the bags from her trunk.

Jogging to her, I give her a hand, wrapping an arm around a paper bag of groceries.

"Hey! Thanks!" She smiles, grabbing one more bag. God, it's good to see her again. I slam the hood shut and eye her tight little body as she sashays inside.

"I nearly had to grab an Uber. My car was giving me problems. It's why I'm so late." She exhales, and my eyes widen at her statement.

"Why would you take a fucking Uber?" I snap.

She shrugs. "So I could get here. I'm already going to have to make this a flying visit. My father wants me home tonight, Sebastian. I'm sorry." Her tone is soft, but there's something in her eyes: deceit. Does he really expect her, or is she making an excuse not to be with me?

"What? Why?" I bark. Her eyes widen at my outburst. "You were going to stay over. It was going to be perfect," I seethe. Dropping my bags, I grip her by the elbow and turn her to face me.

"Don't do this, Sabella," I exhale.

ENVY

"Jesus, Sebastian. It's not like it was set in stone. You know how my family is." She shifts on her feet, clearly uncomfortable.

Taking a deep breath, I try to control myself. "It's just...I care about you and wanted us to have some time together." My tone is softer, and her lips turn up in a tight smile.

"Well, let's not waste the time we do have arguing." She does this cute little nod thing and turns on her heel. "Now, come on, let's do some cooking!"

Inside the light of the house, I get a full look at her. She's wearing a white, soft-looking sweater with a flower printed skirt that tickles her thighs just right. She's reminds me of a young Liv Taylor. Soft spoken, classy, and just fucking beautiful in every way.

She slows her steps, taking in the place.

"It's so homey in here. I love it," she admires.

"Thank you." I slide my hands into my pockets, eyeing her up and down. I wish I could say fuck the food and fuck her.

Her eyes finally fall to mine, and that light, happy feeling fills me up—the one I only get around her.

"You didn't have to bring groceries. I would have picked up whatever you needed, babe."

She looks into the top of one of her bags.

"I didn't mind. I actually enjoy going to the market." She shrugs, and the mental image of her peeking into a deep freezer, her skirt riding up just a little too far, has me seconds away from applying to work at said market.

Clearing my throat, I gesture my hand toward my kitchen.

She prances off and starts unpacking things onto the

half island.

"I hope you like Caprese chicken," she says, her voice hopeful.

"If you're making it, I will." I lay on the charm. I have no fucking clue what Caprese chicken is.

Setting some greens down, her cheeks flush.

"Do you know how to cook?" she asks.

I open my mouth, then close it quickly.

"No," I laugh, making her giggle.

"Well, tonight you will! It's good to have a friend to share my cooking skills with." She smiles. Turning, she tugs a knife free of its block and starts to cut the greenery. There's that word again. *Friend*.

"We want to mince it, like this." She chops and slices through it with ease. "Come over here," she says.

Stepping up behind her, I rest my hands on top of hers, my face so close, my lips brush against her ear. She hesitates. She hadn't expected me to do that.

"Like this," I whisper against her ear. Her hands falter, her face turning just so as I take over the knife. My dick is as hard as rock in my jeans. There's no way she can't feel it.

"Yes," she mutters, but the end of the word is lost.

"Who taught you how to cook, Sabella?"

"The nannies were useless and Sammy used to go hungry at times to make sure my belly was full, so I learned how to cook. I mean, someone had to feed Sammy a meal or he would have starved to death." She shrugs, looking back down at our work. Hearing she cooked for her brother sparks a fire inside me I don't like. I know they're brother and sister, but I want every drop of Sabella's attention from here on out. No Sam. Just her and me. Together. My dick throbs and my head spins.

She suddenly tenses within my hold and pulls some tomatoes free of the bag.

Taking a step back, I let her do her thing, but I don't want to. I'm so infatuated with her, I could care less about ever eating again.

I could be a starving man and I'd survive so long as I had her.

Sabella. Sabella. Sabella. Her name runs circles around my mind. Her scent intoxicates me.

"These we need to cook," she informs with a soft smile, but I don't care about the fucking tomatoes. I want her. I need her. Now.

I slap them out of her hand, and her eyes widen.

"Sebastian!" she calls out in surprise.

But my name on her lips only spurs me on. Gripping her soft thighs, I lift her and plop her down on the chopped greens, knocking the knife to the floor.

"Sebastian!" she giggles, but it's not real amusement; it's mixed with unease.

She's fearful of me, and that should make me back off, but it doesn't. It spurs me on. Her fear is an even bigger aphrodisiac to me.

"Fuck the tomatoes. The only thing I want is you," I tell her. Leaning forward, I press my lips to hers. She tries to resist, fighting against my rough embrace at first before finally submitting. She palms my face and kisses me back, fueling my love for her. I need her right fucking now.

My hands roam up her thighs, touching, feeling, fucking taking. I deepen the kiss, prying her lips to part with a flick of my tongue. She opens up for me, and I sigh into her, caressing her tongue with my own.

Fuck, even her mouth is sweet. I never want to let her

go. Ever.

She moans, widening her legs for me. Growling, I dig my fingers into her ass and pull her sweet little cunt closer to me. The music from the stereo, "Cry Little Sister" by McMahon, heard above our hard pants takes hold of my soul as I dive into what I've been longing for. Sweet Sabella.

As soon as the heat from my cock presses against her, she freezes.

"Wait! Wait." She exhales on a labored breath. "I can't do this!"

"Yes, you can. Don't fight it," I whisper against her collarbone, smelling her, tasting her.

"I..." She lets me kiss her again, and I grind my dick onto her clit a little harder. "Look at me," I demand, wanting to see those gray eyes glaze over with lust.

"Sebastian, I..." Innocence falls from her lips, and I eat it up, kissing her insecurities away.

She moans against my mouth, and I take that as the green light, beginning to tug at her dainty skirt.

"Wait." She presses a hand against my chest hard, forcing me back.

Fucking teasing my restraint.

"Don't fight it. Let me love you, Sabella," I urge, moving in again. Can't she see we're perfect for each other? Can't she feel what I'm feeling for Christ's sake?

"I can't," she murmurs.

"Why?" I beg, kissing her again.

"I'm just not ready for this, and Sam is your friend."

"Fuck Sam. We can run away. Just you and me. Leave Sam and everyone behind." Words fall from my mouth faster than I can register what the hell I'm saying, but I wouldn't take any of it back. I mean it.

"Wait, what?" She's shoving at me now and shaking her head. "No, I can't leave Sammy!" She is completely resisting now, forcing her legs to close. No! This isn't what I wanted.

Anger begins to pulse in my neck, my hand sliding up her throat before moving to grip her hair.

"Yes, you can. For me, you can. You love me, Sabella." I demand it of her.

"I don't," she bites out, gaining strength with her resistance. "Stop it, Sebastian. That is enough!" She shoves me back hard, and my eyes widen like a wounded dog.

Wiping the spit from my mouth, I eye her angrily. My chest feels hollow and full of abandonment as it dawns on me that Sabella may not even care about me.

"Why, why can't you love me like Rhett loves Chastity, or Sam and Patience?" My voice rises, and I slam my fist on the counter still glaring at her.

"Sammy and who?" Her brow crashes down. She looks shocked Sam has a girlfriend, but that's not the point. She's focusing on the wrong fucking thing.

"Me! I need you to love me, Sabella! To want to be with me! I got you a fucking rose!" I point to the flower sitting behind her, one petal already fallen to its death.

She turns, her eyes grazing over the lone rose.

"It's beautiful, Sebastian, but I'm just...I'm not ready to love anyone right now."

"What?" I bite out. She faces me, and all I see is black mist clouding my vision. The sting of defeat poisons my senses, infecting my stability.

"I don't want a relationship with you. I'm sorry if I gave you that impression. You make it hard to just be your friend, and that's all I want to be." She hesitates, looking anxious. But I'm not ready to give up on us.

She just needs reminding. I have to show her how good I can make it for her. How much I fucking love her. Grabbing her around the waist, I pull her from the counter roughly.

"No, Sebastian. What the hell are you doing?" she squeals, but it's okay. She just needs to see. To feel. Grabbing her by the shoulders, I shake her, my heart breaking at my own feet. I have everything—but her.

The brothers. The family. The house. The car. The world at my fucking fingertips. I just need her.

"I just need you, Sabella! You're the last key to it all!" I bite out.

Her eyes go wide. She's frightened. But I don't care. I need her to love me—and she will.

"Sebastian, you're hurting me!" she cries, struggling in my hold.

"Shhh. Just let me love you," I plead, kissing her cheek, her neck, down the valley of her tits.

"You're hurting me! Stop it." She's slapping at me now, struggling in my grip.

"I love you, Sabella!"

"No!" she snaps.

My hands slide up and around her neck. Her mouth parts as wide as her eyes. She struggles, and we stumble and fall to the floor with a soft thud. Air whooshes from her, stunning her briefly, and it gives me time to kiss her lips. *I'm going to show you so much love, baby.*

She attempts to slap at my hands, she's thrashing, but I tighten my hold on her throat once more. Her eyes expand impossibly large, her creamy skin turning a pretty pale color. "Yeah, baby. Just...shhh."

Lust, wrath, pride, greed, gluttony—I feel all my brothers' sins coursing through me, swirling inside me like a tornado ripping everything apart and raining down chaos.

"I'm not going to hurt you. I'd never fucking hurt you, Sab."

Black. Black. Black. As I try to consume every inch of my sweet, fighting Sabella, my mind gets sucked into the void. Into the sheer madness. Screams. Begging. It's all a cacophony in my dark mind. All I feel right now is her. Mine. Mine. Mine. Pain slices across my arm, making me jolt back. My eyes widen as I take in the small knife coming at me again. I'm yanked from my inner wildness and thrust back into the present. With a surge of energy, she shifts, knocking me off-kilter.

"Bastard! Get off me! Stay back!"

She glares at me, tears trailing down her cheeks as she bares the knife like a monster. Her hair is wild and her body bruised as she attempts to shuffle backwards.

Fucking traitorous bitch!

I reach for her, and she swipes it in my direction. "Stay back!" she screams, waving the knife like a crazy fucking person.

"You bastard!" she chokes, flaying the fucking thing at me. "Don't touch me! Don't touch me! I hate you! I hate you!" she stammers on sobbed breaths.

All I can think about is the rejection suffocating my self-worth. Why is she doing this to me—to us?

Doesn't she see? I need her to make me a better person. Without her, I'm nothing. We're meant to be, and she's fucking ruining it all. I reach for her quickly and grab her wrist. I twist it until I hear a pop and she drops the knife, howling in pain.

"You made me fucking do that," I bark. She manages to move farther away from me and attempts to get up and flee.

"Get back here!" Jumping up, I'm on her in seconds. Grabbing at her ankle, I drag her backwards, and she screams as she kicks out at me. Red rage saturates my body in its wrath as her foot hits me in the jaw and I'm almost stunned. "Fuck!" I yell.

This is all going so fucking wrong.

"Why did you do this? Why!" I roar, trapping her beneath me again.

Perhaps I can still make this all okay.

She's not fighting back anymore.

"Sabella, I'm sorry. I didn't mean to frighten you."

She's not moving or talking.

"Sabella?"

Blinking, I come to, pulling my hands away from her. Blood drips from my arm like a broken faucet, and it's then I realize I'm holding the knife in my hand.

"Sabella…" I move off her, but she's still.

"Sabella, stop it. Get up," I growl. Nothing.

Her sweater seeps with pools of red. It's looks like spilled ink spreading out from tiny little slashes. Holy shit, what did I do?

Dropping the knife to the floor like it's handle is on fire, I crawl to her and turn her over.

Her beautiful gray eyes stare dead ahead, no glimpse of life in them.

No. No. No. Oh, shit. Why did you make me do this?

Standing, I run my hands through my hair, trying to

gain my senses back. Fuck. She's dead. I begin to panic.

Pacing, I can't stop looking at the body lying on my kitchen floor, blood creeping from beneath her like a chalk outline. She's fucking gone. All she had to do was love me.

"Am I that hard to love?" I plead with her. "Why did you do this?" Tears begin to fill my eyes. I wanted to love her. We would have been great. We would have been a family.

Falling to my knees, I cradle her in my arms and kiss her blue lips. Her skin is paling and she's getting cold already.

"Wake up, baby. I'm sorry," I whisper, willing her to take a deep breath. But she doesn't. I destroyed my happiness. She was too much for me. I was a rough kid trying to handle a fairy he only heard about in storybooks. The realization that I could be happy was blinding.

Brushing the hair from her face, I wonder who I should call. An ambulance? My uncle? The Elite?

I sniffle, knowing I can't call anyone. I'll go to jail, or The Elite will abandon me for hurting one of our own. Sam will kill me. I can't lose my brotherhood. It's all I have left now.

I have to get rid of her body. I nod to myself. Yes, I have to.

I have to let her go.

Say goodbye.

I hate it—she deserves better than this—but it's the only way.

I'll take her to the swamp behind God's parents' house, the same place we went to dispose of Rhett's dad before we found out he wasn't dead. A presence takes over me. Shaking out my shoulders, I crack my neck. The familiar darkness that dwells inside when Sabella isn't around takes control.

A sound chirps from her cell phone. I drop her and go to see who the fuck is texting her at night. It's from her father, demanding to know where she is.

Fuck.

I need my hoodie to do the job, but it's at the dorms. I have to get it, and then take care of my mess. Looking down at myself, I cringe. Shower first.

Deadweight is no joke. Sab is a petite girl, but fuck, her body is heavy. I shift the wrapped body again over my shoulder and walk to the door. Clicking the button to open her trunk, I dump her inside.

This could have been so different. She caused this. It's not my fault.

Locking up the house, I drive her car to the marshes near God's parents' house. The terrain tests her small car, and when the wheels stick, I stop and carry her the rest of the way.

There's a pit in my gut when I drop her down and give her body a kick. It's so dark, I can barely see if she's submerging. I don't have time to wait for any light or to go back and get a torch. Sam will be looking for her by now. I have to dump her car, but not here, that will lead them to her body. Fuck. Jumping in the car, I drive it halfway toward the grocery store. If she's on their cameras, they'll search this route, and then it looks like she didn't make it to me.

I'm a fucking genius.

ENVY

Blood is beginning to seep through the bandage I put on my wound. It needs stitches, but I can't risk going to the hospital. Maybe superglue will work. It doesn't hurt much, surprisingly.

Taking off at a steady jog, making it home in twenty minutes.

The house looks like a horror movie.

Throwing towels on the floor, I use my foot to soak up Sabella's blood. The white cotton bleeds into a work of abstract art. This evening didn't go as I planned at all.

My phone dings in my back pocket, and I pull it out to see who the fuck it is.

Lillian: Why is Samuel here with Patience? Get to the school now and get rid of him. Don't fuck this up if you know what's good for you.

Shit. Talk about fucking bad timing.

I consider not going—I have a lot of shit to do—but enduring Lillian's wrath won't work out well for me. She could take everything else away—my brotherhood, my Elite. I can't lose those as well.

Shoving my phone back in my pants, I wash my hands, change my shirt, and head out.

My hands are shaking, the look of Sab's pale face staining my vision. Finally, in the parking lot, I spot Sam and head over to him. I knock on the window.

"I won't be alone. He'll be there to stop it." She points at me.

They both look up at me, and I go wide-eyed realizing I just walked in on a conversation. They want me to do something, and from the looks on their faces, it's not going to be easy. Sam gets out of the car, and I take a step back. I don't have time for this shit. I have a mess to clean up back home.

"You think you can do it?" Sam asks me. Fuck, I can't even look him in the eyes right now. Every time I do, I see Sab. I'm not entirely sure what he's going on about, but I agree to whatever he's asking anyway.

"Yeah, of course. I've got your back." I shrug, looking to the ground. Anything he needs, I have his back—and he knows that. I just can't have his back when it comes to his sister. I'm a bad friend, for sure. Maybe we'll still be able to have family barbeques one day, though. There's gotta be a girl for me somewhere out there, right?

A beautiful red Ferrari pulls into the parking lot, and Sam's face goes hard. Judging by the older man behind the wheel, this must be the legendary asshole father Sam goes on about. I wonder if he's as angry as Sam is half the time.

"I'll be fine, won't I?" Patience says to me, her doe eyes looking up to me like I'm her hero. If only she knew. Shaking the unease of tonight's events, I throw my arm around Patience's small frame.

"Of course!" I agree. And I want that to be the truth. Sam is my brother and I've already taken enough from him tonight, but I'm so preoccupied with thoughts of Sabella and the shit I still need to clean up, I worry I'm not coming across as sincere. I can do this, for my brother.

Sam starts that romantic shit with her, and it makes me think of what I don't and won't have. What I just lost. What Sabella destroyed. My dream of having a woman by my side is slowly being digested in the gut of alligators. I swallow hard just thinking about it—about her. She was such a beauty too. I don't see me getting over Sabella as quickly as the girls before her.

"You!" Sam points at me. I look at him, and he starts throwing threats my way. If anything happens to his girl, it'll be my ass, blah, blah, blah. I just nod. My head is too filled with guilt and secrets of his sister to acknowledge the task at hand. I'm really not the brother for the job, but I can't tell him that. He needs me.

Sam reluctantly gets in his dad's car, and Patience and I turn away.

"Wait, where is Sam going?" I ask, just realizing he's leaving.

Patience looks over her shoulder. "Um…"

"It doesn't matter. Just tell me the plan," I say, needing her to explain what it is I'm doing so I can get back to my place.

"We just need to make the dean look like a pervert, that he's coming onto students, so Sam's task can be complete. I need you to come in and stop the dean before anything terrible happens to me. Can you do that?"

"We've got this." I flick my nose and keep my eyes straight ahead.

Entering the dean's corridor, Patience inhales a deep breath and knocks on the door. She's nervous. I can practically smell the fear dripping from her skin.

She slips into the office when a man's voice accepts entry.

Leaning against the wall, I go to fidget with my watch, but realize it's missing. What the fuck? I must have taken it off back home when I washed my hands. Damn. I need a drink. I need sleep too. I need a lot of things. I hear the mumble of Patience and the dean talking, but nothing much else.

My phone buzzes, making me jump. Jerking it out of my pocket, I find Lillian calling me.

"What?" I snap.

"You can leave now. Get back to whatever task had you held up," she says, her tone cold.

"I can't leave, Patience is…"

"Don't make me tell you again, Sebastian, unless you want me to send your brothers to your new place. Who knows what secrets they might uncover."

Fuck!

"Leave, now," she says and hangs up.

Jumping in my car, I peel out of the parking lot just as my phone chirps again. This time it's Rhett.

"Where are you?"

"I'm just taking off. I need to do something. I left Sam's girl at the college."

With that, I end the call. I can't focus on anything right now but covering up what I've just done. I make it back to my house, and there's no fucking trace of the shit I left here. No bloody towels—no fucking nothing—and my watch is nowhere to be found.

This is Lillian—the fucking Elite. They must have cameras in this place, and now they know what I've done.

My stomach tanks, and I feel like I'm going to throw up. My head is spinning, and I stumble backwards to lean against the kitchen counter before I fall over.

My cell goes off, making me jump out of my skin.

"What!" I bark.

"Dude, Sabella is missing. They found her car with blood in it. We're getting together to find her. You want to meet us in the college parking lot?" Micah speaks quickly into the phone.

My chest seizes, my entire body ablaze with panic. Fuck, that was fast.

"Y-Yeah," I nervously reply. Before I hang up, I'm already running back to my car.

What if they find her body? What if she wasn't dead?

Biting my lip, I know I need to go make sure she's gone—that the swamp took care of my dirty work.

VII

UINCENDUM NATUS

TWENTY-ONE

My car only makes it so far into the wet marshland before I have to stomp through the mud to get to where I took the body. It smells out here, and it's dark. The only light from the lone moon above casts a hopeless glare across the water. Even with that, it's hard to see. Using my fingers, I spread them through the water, startling an alligator close by. The familiar hissing sound before a snap is heard as it submerges into the murky water. From the looks of it, there's about four gators.

I swallow, taking the deep waters in one more time. I don't see a trace of Sab's body. It saddens me it came to this, that we couldn't love each other the way I wanted. Turning, I rub my forehead and go back to my car, scraping my shoes along the terrain to get some mud off.

In my car, I grab a shirt from the backseat and rub at

my pants in attempt to dry them off.

What a fucking night.

Heading back to campus, all I can think about is how am I going to lie to my brothers and act like I don't know where Sabella is? How can I lie to Sam? Being in The Elite is proving to be more intense than I thought. And what the hell will Lillian want from me now? She fucking knows what I've done.

Finally getting to campus, there are police lights everywhere and people standing around recording. My heart stops.

They know it was me. They know what I've done.

I have half a mind to drive away. Just fucking drive and not come back, but then I think of Sabella's beautiful gray eyes and the way they stared up at me. They way she felt wrapped around me. We could have been something fucking special.

I know I can't run from this. I have to own up to the shit I've done.

I look across at the chaos, watching as Sam is walked out of the school in cuffs, and then it hits me how badly today has really gone. I have completely fucked up.

Patience! Throwing my car in park, I run to the scene, finding my brothers surrounding a cop car, Sam shoved in the backseat.

Trying to keep my cool, I swallow the lump in my throat, guilt pressuring me to the point of barely breathing. I fucked up. I fucked up so bad. Rush turns and looks at me, his arms crossed.

"Patience was raped and Sam lost his shit, brother."

My mouth parts. I let this happen. I fucking did this.

Stepping out the way of cops, I find myself next to

Mason. He turns and looks at me with hard eyes.

"Where the fuck have you been?" his tone cut-throat. I don't answer. How can I? Where do I even begin?

His eyes fall to my hands, and he takes a step back.

"Don't tell me that's what I think it is, man." I twitch my blood-stained hands, the evidence of my sins clear as day.

"I cut myself. That's why I had to leave," I lie, and he frowns.

"You okay?"

No. "Yeah. Why is Sam being arrested?"

My heart is going to rip from my chest as the anxiety continues to spike. "He beat the shit outta the dean," he tells me.

I can't even look at him right now. I can't look at any of my brothers. Turning my gaze anywhere but at him, I find fucking Lillian stalking behind an ambulance, her face busted up. What the hell happened when I left? I can't help but feel she set this whole thing up. She wanted me to fail, and I did. I was led into a trap by the goddamn devil herself.

Patience is crying and telling Sam it's going to be ok. Red and blue lights are flashing, highlighting everything. Crowds are gathering to see what's happening—and all I can think about is the mud all over me and the guilt written on my face.

"I've fucked up so bad," I mutter.

"Sebastian, talk to me. What did she make you do?" Mason pushes for me to give him anything, but I can't. I feel like I'm watching the scene, but not really a part of it.

"Wrath's going to kill me." My voice cracks with emotion. Realization that I've lost everything in a matter of minutes heavy on my shoulders. Lillian's eyes cut through the crowd and pin me to the spot, a smirk tilting up her blood-covered lips. She got what she wanted, but where does that leave me?

"Why is Lillian bleeding?" I croak.

Mason follows my gaze and snorts. "Sam head-butted her. Bitch deserves way fucking more. She's a snake, poison to the core. She will use you up and spit you out, so if she's made you do something, just tell us so we can help you. You're our brother."

No, I'm not, though. Olly was. Fuck, I hate myself right now. I've ruined my own life.

Moving toward the car, Mason calls out, "Samuel," and nods over to God, who tilts his head and says, "I'll handle it."

The police officer climbs in the car and starts the engine. Mason goes over to comfort Patience, who's sobbing. "We'll sort this, brother," he reassures Sam as the car begins to pull away. Sam's eyes collide with mine, narrowing, seeking me out amongst our brothers. I school my features so he can't read me. He nods his head at me, the intensity of his glare making me falter. His scolding dead eyes land right on me. He's speaking to me without saying a word.

Warning me.

Threating.

A motherfucking promise.

He's coming for me.

And I fucking deserve his wrath.

Going to see Sam was a bad idea, but I needed to see him to let him know I didn't mean it.

I get back to my house and check my cell, but none of my brothers have reached out; they're done with me. I let Sam down. Opening the front door, I walk in and chuck my keys down on the coffee table, but freeze when I see a huge figure standing in my living room.

"Who the fuck are you?" I growl.

When he turns, the moonlight bleeding through the window highlights his face and I recognize him from media photos. Malcom Benedict the Third. Lillian's brother.

"What do you want?" I demand, walking toward the kitchen to grab a knife.

It's then I see he isn't alone. "I'm just here to fix a mistake my sister made. You see, Mr. Westbrook, she's been making a lot of those lately. If I didn't know better, I'd say she's up to something." He nudges his chin, giving his henchmen the cue to surround me.

"She's a fucking bitch," I snap, and he narrows his eyes on me. Walking across the room, he swipes his finger along the counter, then burrows his hand in his pocket, pulling out my fucking watch! "Do you know how easy it is for me to clean house? You left this in Miss Sabella's car, along with your blood—amateur for someone who has killed before," he tuts.

"So, you're going to have me arrested?" I scowl. Snorting, he shakes his head in amusement.

"And have it known what a mess my sister made by allowing a criminal's heir to breach The Elite and murder a legitimate member's sister? I think not."

"Then what?" I try to move, but the guys surrounding me close in, restricting me completely.

ENVY

The big bastard picks up my watch and begins rubbing his thumb over the face.

"No one fucks with my family's legacy. The Elite was formed for exactly that purpose. Power. Status. Invisibility. Only the best is initiated. Far from the adolescent fuck-up like you. Lillian thought she could use you to do her bidding, but my rogue of a sister let her guard down. Allowing you to infiltrate her files and upload your name was a mistake we're now paying for. I'll give you props, Mr. Westbrook—no one else has gotten this close to The Elite. Lillian thinks I'm unaware of her little games to try to gain power, but she's more of a fool than you are. In the end, she will always need me to come clean up her mistakes, and that's all you are—an error in her judgment."

It's the first time I've ever been this nervous and feel out of my comfort zone.

"My uncle…" I start, but his laughter shuts me down.

"Your uncle is an ant compared to me, boy. No one gets away with making a mockery of The Elite. I'll bury your sins and you with them. Now, lets move this along, shall we? I have to go have a little talk with my darling sister." Dropping my watch to the floor, he stomps on it. I struggle to break free.

"Don't," I beg.

Picking up the broken pieces, he smirks and stuffs it in my pocket. "Time has stopped for you, boy."

Hands grab at me, and I try to fight them off, but then a pinprick goes into my arm. Before I know what's happening, darkness steals my thoughts.

VII

U I N C E N D U M   N A T U S

EPILOGUE

My mouth is dry, and my head hurts. Licking my lips, I turn on my side. Only…I can't move. My eyes struggle to open, and I notice I'm not in my bed. I'm in some room with gray walls, the smell of alcohol and apples unfamiliar. Where the fuck am I?

I lift my arms in a panic. I'm restrained to a bed with only a white, threadbare sheet beneath me. I jerk again.

"What the fuck?" I murmur. The bed rocks at my attempted fight. The clothes I went to bed in last night are gone, replaced with blue scrub-like pants and a shirt.

"Hello!" My voice echoes throughout the room.

A woman peeks through the glass window on the only door. It clicks before she enters.

She's young, wearing bright red scrubs.

"Where am I?" I snap, the flesh of my wrist smarting

from the leather straps strangling them.

"Hi there, Mr. Westbrook. I'm Nori. How are you this afternoon?"

"Where the fuck am I?" I ask again. "Am I in a hospital?"

She tucks her hands inside of the front pockets of her top.

"Um, yeah. You're in a hospital…of sorts." She smiles, her lips matching her outfit.

"What happened?" I start to ease up, knowing I'm safe. Although, I don't remember getting hurt. Last thing I remember is … fuck, The Elite. Lillian's brother.

"That's something you and your doctor will talk about, I'm sure." She lays a forgiving hand on my bruised wrist, and I feel that touch all the way through my body. It's warm against my cold skin. My eyes snap to hers. They're blue, deep blue.

"From what I read from your file, it seems as if you've been severely hallucinating," she whispers, looking over her shoulder in worry.

Hallucinations? That can't be right. That's a lie.

"Who put me in here?"

"Some caring friends admitted you, and your counselor signed off on it."

"Friends? I don't have any—"

The Elite. They did this. But was it because of Sabella, or because I fucked over Sam with Patience and got his girl raped? Probably both.

Lifting my head, I slam it back down.

"Fuck!"

I screwed this all up. My only chance of having a normal life and I ruined it.

I slam my head back again.

"Fuck!"

And again.

And again.

"Sebastian!" Nori begins to panic, her arms in the air, trying to calm me.

"Fuck. Fuck!" I jerk at my restraints, my legs kicking and neck aching from thrashing my head about. My brothers abandoned me. Sabella is dead. No doubt my uncle wants nothing to do with me now either. I have no one to love me. I'm alone. I've always been alone.

Nori runs out of the room, only to return seconds later with a large man in tow.

"All right, Sebastian. Deep breath, honey!" She raises a needle with a vial at the tip, the syringe sucking in a clear liquid.

The man holds down my upper arm, and Nori slams the needle in.

"There, there." She smiles, rubbing the injection site.

My whole body feels fuzzy, and a happiness blankets my soul—a calmness I've never felt before.

Blinking slowly, I look to Nori. Her caring eyes gaze back at me with concern.

"I hate getting new guys in." The beefy dude lets go of me and steps back. He wraps his arms around Nori, and she giggles.

"No!" I slur. They can't be together. She's too caring, too sweet. I need her more than anyone right now.

"Not right here, Pep." She slaps him away. My whole body instantly feels warm with rage, wanting her, needing that female companionship. Why can't I have someone? Why does God constantly put happy couples in front of me like this?

Then, I swim in a deep blackness that can only be compared to what death must feel like. I'm knocked out.

Rush, Sam, Micah, Rhett, God, and Mason all come into my nightmare, standing around me in cloaks of black. I can't see their faces, but I can feel their anguish.

"Brothers, please!" I raise a hand, begging them to understand where I'm coming from.

"You've betrayed us, brother. Broke an oath, and now...The Elite must teach you." The words echo in my head like a bad prayer.

Waking up, my mouth is dry again, and my body feels tense. I'm sitting in a wheelchair in a room full of strangers. Blue scrubs again. A blue robe.

"What the fuck is in that stuff?" I ask myself, looking about the room. The staff wearing red stand out like alarming flags. You can't miss them.

Some people are playing cards at a circular table. Some watch TV in the corner. There's just a lot of fucking people. Weird people. My eyes drag to a clock on the wall, the date next to it. Wait, what the fuck? "The date's wrong," I bark out, gaining attention.

"Hey, Sebastian. How are you feeling today?" Nori asks, her fire engine lipstick making my dick hard in my state of lethargy. She's a lot like Sabella in a way, her caring, fuck-tease nature.

"The date, it's wrong. I've only been here a day or two."

Offering me a pity smile, she shakes her head. "No, you've been here weeks, Sebastian."

No fucking way.

"Why am I here?" I mumble. *Where the hell is this fucking place?*

"It's where you belong."

No. I reach for her and pull her to me, my hand snaking around her neck. "No, it fucking isn't. Why am I here?" I growl, and her eyes narrow. There's no fear on her features.

"Mr. Benedict says you're ours now. We don't ask questions—and you shouldn't either." She smirks, then a needle prick hits my neck while some dude grabs my wrists from behind and forces me to release Nori. The calm trickles back in and I'm floating again

Time passes slow in here. Being on and off the meds makes everything feel foreign. Prison would have been better than this.

"Open," Nori tells me. I open my mouth and lift my tongue to show her I swallowed the pills she fed me.

"Are you up for some company?" she asks, all peppy.

My eyes widen. "Someone is here to see me?"

"Yes, a Micah is here." She frowns, looking over her clipboard.

She walks over to the door before pressing a button on the wall and letting herself out. A few minutes later, the door clicks back open, and there is my fucking brother Micah. He looks fresh, alive from the other side of this fucking cage. I blink a few times, the drugs ever heavy in my system. His image sways and disappears, just like the rest of the brothers in my dreams the last few days. *They're not real.*

"Hey, brother…" he whispers, looking me over with pity in his eyes.

"Micah?"

He steps forward. "Yeah, bro, it's me."

I practically throw myself at him, wrapping him up in a hug. "It's good to see someone from the outside."

"Yeah, I bet. With Sabella still missing, things are still all up in the air," he tells me, patting my back.

My body solidifies at his words. *Is he really here? Sabella…*

He moves away, but his eyes never leave mine.

"Bro, is there something bothering you?" he asks, studying me.

I sit my ass back down, the drugs making me all woozy. "Why did you come and see me, Micah?" I ask, keeping the slur from my words.

"You want me to bullshit, or you want me to tell the truth?"

"The truth."

"Truth, huh? Funny, because that's exactly why I came here." His words sound distant, and I know I'm fucking dreaming. He's not really here. Sab's shadowy figure appears, haunting me in my cell.

"I didn't mean to take it that far," I plead with her.

"You didn't mean to *what?*"

I can hear noise and feel my lips moving, but everything is coming out without permission and I can't get a hold of my words.

"Why?" I hear Micah ask.

"Because I envied her." *Them—everyone.*

My ears rings, my head pounding, and I have to rest it on my palm to steady myself.

A clanking of my door closing makes me startle. I search the room for Micah, for Sabella, for anyone, but I'm alone again—just me and my crazed thoughts.

I hate this fucking place. People come and go, but not me.

"You're new," some old cunt barks at me. "I said, are you new?" she repeats. She has raggedy red hair, and a voice that sounds like she's been smoking non-stop for the last twenty years.

I shift uncomfortably.

"My stay will be short," I snap, rubbing my wrist where my watch usually is. *And I'm not fucking new, I've been here way too long already.*

She laughs.

"No, it won't. I can tell you're not one of them." She points to a guy jerking off in a corner, some woman next to him using his cum that splatted onto his pants to glue her paper flowers to her own scrubs.

"Exactly why I'll be out," I murmur, not wanting to talk to her.

"Exactly why you ain't leaving, handsome. Someone put you in here for a reason, and you ain't getting out." She laughs, wheeling herself to the windows behind us. That cackle makes me shrink back into my chair. Someone stole that crazy bitch off a farm somewhere.

Jesus, this place is fucked.

"I want Jell-O! I want Jell-O!" a man yells, unreasonably loud, grabbing my attention from the rest of the patients.

"All right, Alfred. I'm getting it." That voice. Turning my head to the side, I find Nori unlocking a room, smiling at the Alfred guy who begins to clap and jump up and down. He's older than me, much older by the looks of his balding.

Seconds later, Nori is pushing out a cart full of Jell-O in an array of colors.

"Here you are. Now, no taking anyone else's this time!" she scolds, handing him a lime flavored treat.

She passes out cup after cup, a smile on her face with every giving. Who is this woman? How is she so nice to a bunch of crazies?

Her eyes hit mine, and something inside me lights up. *Sabella*....

Sashaying toward me, she hands me a cup of purple Jell-O. It's cold, and appetizing, *but I'd rather have you, Nori.*

"Would you like one, Sebastian?"

Smiling, I take it from her.

"How long have you worked here, Nori?"

"Long enough.." She places her hands on her hips. Fuck, I'm so lonely. She's perfect.

"Oh, I have something that's long enough." I wink, and I notice the lust flash across her ocean eyes.

"You're a charmer, aren't you?" She smirks, tucking a stray brown hair behind her ear.

Biting my lip, I lower my head, my eyes at half-mast.

"Oh, you have no idea."

"Oh, I think I do." She raises a brow and waltzes off.

Challenge accepted.

"Sebastian!" she calls over her shoulder, making my dick jerk.

"What?" I smirk, waiting for her to tell me to meet her in the office for a private one on one. But her next words make me freeze.

"Your brothers are here for you."

"What?"

"You heard me." She folds her arms and narrows her gaze on me from across the room.

"Which one?" I ask, hearing the trepidation in my own voice.

"All of them."

THE END

ACKNOWLEDGEMENTS

I don't even know where to start. This book was so much fun to write, I have no regrets! Sebastian is a character that has been dying to get out and he did so without remorse!

Big thank you to Ker Dukey for asking me to pitch in my crazy side for this amazing project! This book couldn't have made it to where it is without her, Holly, K Webster, Claire, Amo, and Giana. We are a team, and it showed! This entire series was brilliant!

I am so thankful for everyone pitching in and sharing the series! Your support and love is very much appreciated! Be a new reader, or one that has been with me since the start I hope you enjoy everything M.N. Forgy! I love reviews!

STALK THE AUTHOR

Stalk her on Facebook:
www.facebook.com/Author-MN-Forgy-625362330873655

Stalk her on Instagram:
www.instagram.com/mnforgyauthor

Sign up for her newsletter:
mnforgy.com/newsletter

MORE FROM M.N. FORGY

42931602R00099

Made in the USA
Middletown, DE
21 April 2019